By Kaylea Prime

Tears of Flame

<u>Novels</u>
A Spark From Embers

<u>Novellas</u>
A Ballad of Hate and Hope
A Tragedy of Sacrifice

KAYLEA
PRIME

A TRAGEDY OF SACRIFICE

FROM THE WORLD
OF TEARS OF
FLAME

Cover design by Miblart

Interior Design by Kaylea Prime

Quill Chapter Heading Image by rawpixel.com on Freepik

Cauldron and Celestial Chapter Heading images by StarGlade Vintage on Pixabay

First edition: October 2024

ISBN 978-1-7380885-5-3 (hardcover)

ISBN 978-1-7380885-6-0 (paperback)

ISBN 978-1-7380885-7-7 (ebook)

www.kayleaprime.com

For Candace and Tamara.
Sisters by blood, but also my sisterhood, my chosen coven, and some of the most powerful women capable of inspiring change that I know.

North Western
Hemisphere of Arwe
NIROSULA
CARMELLE

CENTRAL CARMELLE
CARENTH-HILD
BELLAND
Tulandi
Carenthia
Steepleton
Yena Aisis
Voita Woods
Aganeni
Edgewater
MELLOTH
Athatairs
Helgur
Calessar
Gap of Talari
TOLOTANTEAU
FIRNETH LOMIN
Nethteneni
Tariq
LOTHILYA
Velleneni
Aspengrove Island
CAR
Dharmae

ÉALOTH
Evírn Aisis
Evíar
VANDO
ORINLOTH
DÉLUREN
Sefarú River
Tor Niro
Nironení
Tor Yena
Keleb-Sola
TOR
STELLA
LALÍTÉ
NÍRON
VASMORLOTH
ELLE
TANTEAU
Norance Dunes

Contents

Prologue

November 1692, Salem, Massachusetts

Dead leaves crunched beneath the dusting of fresh snow under Gertrude's low-heeled shoes like brittle bones breaking beneath a veil of cobwebbed lace. The curled corners of frosted leaves poking up between snowflakes glittered, and she pulled back the edge of her hood to glance up at the full moon. Tendrils of cloud had been drifting across it since she had sneaked out of her house, and they cast warped shadows across the forest floor. She flitted from shadow to shadow, her long black cloak slithering across the damp mulch mingled with tree roots.

A *crack* splintered the stilted silence, and Gertrude sidestepped behind the bole of a thick pine. Holding her breath, she slowly swivelled her head to peer over her shoulder, her erratic heartbeat skittering behind her rib cage like a terrified mouse.

A black void swallowed the thicket, emptied of movement and sound. No leaves rustled. No creature stirred. Even the moon did not waver as a cloud's wispy fingers scrabbled across its surface, as if it, too, held its breath.

Her imagination must be playing tricks on her again, as it was wont to do.

It was an occupational hazard of being a witch.

At least what the folk of Salem called a witch, though Gertrude had never heard the term before coming to Earth. In the last year, she had heard it decried so often the accusatory shrieks still reverberated between her ears and down her tingling spine every time she considered using her magic again.

But almost two months had passed since the last hangings, and the special court had been dismissed. Her paralyzing fear had begun to ebb, relaxing her tense shoulders and dulling the anxious needles pricking her chest.

She was safe. Her children were safe.

Maybe it was time to answer her magic's lonely lament.

Reining in the wild stallions of her imagination, she scurried to the next tree, following an unseen path her feet had memorized. She fingered the cloth bag fastened at her hip, reassuring herself it was still there. More herbs would need to be gathered and added to the bag before she emerged from these woods tonight, but nestled beneath the clinking bottles, under a bed of stringy lichen, was her greatest treasure—and proof of her sinful, wicked ways, should she ever be caught.

Luckily, catching a real witch was as rare as a man admitting he was wrong. Gertrude didn't even know anyone else with gifts who lived in Salem, unless their concealment enchantments were so powerful they could hide their abilities even from another magic wielder. But the chances were slim.

Wizards didn't just walk through portals every day.

Especially the portal she had.

A cloud shifted, and silver moonlight sliced through the canopy of dying leaves and crooked, snarled branches overhead to reveal a copse of evergreen trees to her right.

Gertrude's heart thrummed, and her long fingers twitched, but she coaxed them to stillness.

Not yet, she instructed the pulsing orb in her core.

Ducking beneath the entangled bell-sleeve branches of two cedars, she entered the copse and began placing bundles of mugwort and thyme around the perimeter. Their protective properties were not as strong as those of the herbs of her world, but with the aid of her treasure, they would suffice. After completing one last inspection of her surroundings to ensure no one lurked nearby, she knelt in the centre of the hexagon she had created. Her uneven fingernails snagged in the tangled curls of her untamed charcoal-grey hair as she lowered the hood of her cloak.

She closed her eyes, breathing in the crisp scent of fresh snow, earthier than she was used to, having never experienced snow at this stage of autumn before—at least not in Salem. The sight of snowflakes cresting waves of burgundy leaves like foam frothing in a sea of blood had been too alluring for Gertrude to resist. The hum of her magic had tingled throughout her whole body, her core tugging her to the woods, to freedom.

Now she embraced the tangled threads of her core, messy and unpredictable and free. Wild, just like her. She bathed in its opalescent light, relishing the thrum of power prickling her veins.

She reached her hand back into the pouch at her waist, plucked her treasure from the depths, and curled it in her fist. Only when she held it aloft in her palm, fingers unfurled, did she open her eyes.

A translucent round stone gleamed in her hand, pearly mist swirling within and emitting a soft glow despite the cloud-veiled moon overhead. She had heard of moonstones on Earth, gems with a pearlescent sheen that older civilizations believed to be chunks of the moon sent by their gods, but her stone was different. Enchanted by Celestial magic, it used captured moonlight to enhance or anchor other magic.

Among her people, the Armindí, it was unique but admired as a useful tool.

In Salem, the independent movement of swirling mist and the inexplicable glow would brand it as the talisman of a witch.

For a woman accused of witchcraft, the only way to prevent a lifeline from coiling into a noose was to be a real witch. Though Gertrude possessed magic, she had never been accused of witchcraft. She wore discretion like plated armour around the small-minded folk of Salem, and guarded against the gaps with chain mail. She couldn't afford to let an arrow pierce through.

During the trials, she had dampened her magic, stifling the thrum of her core so no one could even get a whiff of it.

But sometimes before the trials, when she had stolen away to be alone, she would remove one small piece of the armour.

And seize a thread of her pulsating core.

A single flame sparked amid swirling eddies of snowflakes like a distant star flickering into existence among clouds of dust. Contentment melted the icy corners of Gertrude's heart, and she sank into its warmth, basking in the rays of her core as she directed the flame to the amplifier stone.

Ice or fire.

Sacrifice or happiness.

Opposing words that brushed attracted fingertips but always slid past each other, never aligning.

Despite their resistance, Gertrude had managed to intertwine them.

She had made sacrifices, but not at the expense of her happiness. She had left her home among the Armindí, left her family and everything she knew for the love of a man on Earth. But she was still the same wild spirit; she had retained her powers; and the small sacrifice of hiding her magic was worth the love and happiness she had gained.

The flame enveloped the stone, and Gertrude redirected it to one of the herb bundles, lighting it like a candle. Cupping the flame in her mind, she blew on it like a dandelion and redirected sparks to each bundle, like seeds blowing in the wind, until the entire hexagon was alight. She channelled a thin jet of water from her finger onto the flaming moonstone, and the stone returned to its pearlescent glow, unscathed.

A thin, icy breeze stirred the leaves at Gertrude's feet, and she twisted the gust into a spiral, swirling a dozen leaves up off the ground in a tiny tornado. She dangled the leaves suspended in mid-air like marionettes on strings, limp and lifeless until she tugged the threads of magic tethering them. Her lip snagged on her crooked, crowded front teeth as she grinned, thinking of her children and how delighted they would be to watch a leaf-marionette show. Maybe one day she could perform for them, show them her magic without the fear of fatal consequences.

Up and down the leaves danced, bobbing and gliding and swaying in partnership as she paired them in an elegant swirl. Seamlessly they switched to a more frolicking dance, skipping and bouncing with more gaiety. As the leaves' frivolity intensified, longing clawed at Gertrude's chest, a caged animal desperate for release. Without missing a beat in the leaves' dance, she unbuckled her shoes and slipped them off.

Frigid snow soaked her stockinged feet, but she did not flinch. She laughed, holding her arms out wide, and inhaled deep breaths of icy air. The cold woke her mind and body, setting her spirit free, and she danced with the leaves, twirling and spinning to the tune of fluty wind whistles and stomping foot beats until she teetered with dizziness, cackling at the swaying moon.

A strangled gasp sliced through the echoes of her cackle. Nerves tingled from her fingertips to the nape of her neck, and Gertrude faltered, slipping in the snow. She threw her hands out to catch herself before she ate a mouthful of mulch, and something white fluttered to the ground beside her. Bile rose against the blood pounding at the base of her throat and thrumming in her ears. Pushing herself up on shaky arms, she raised her head to the trees and locked eyes with a short man, his bald head glistening with sweat in the moonlight, beady eyes wide in a face of drooping, loose skin.

Her neighbour John.

John, who always had a quick quip ready when he smelled his favourite sweet bread that she baked, and a stern remark if they were late for church or one of the children misbehaved. John, whose jovial smile reached the corners of his crinkly eyes when he laughed, but whose gaze lingered a fraction too long on her curves when she shuffled past him in the pew aisle. John, whom she sometimes caught peering through the gap in his shuttered windows.

He must have seen her sneak out and followed.

"W-w-witch!" John stammered, voice shrill and raspy.

Leaves rained down on Gertrude's head as she severed the threads of her magic, and her breath sank in her chest like collapsed bread.

He filled his lungs with air and branded her with more force this time. "WITCH!"

Gertrude didn't flinch. Her arms stayed locked, supporting her stiff shoulders and heavy head, her eyes wide and unblinking as she stared at the beads of sweat trickling down John's forehead. The night's icy breath had frozen not only her limbs and face but her thoughts as well. Her numb brain could not process her discovery.

When Gertrude continued to sit there, unmoving in the snow, John's puffy lips curved down in a frown, and his eyes narrowed and widened again in rapid succession. He stumbled back a few steps, evidently unnerved by her lack of reaction. A distant voice in the recesses of her mind pleaded with her to move, to deny the accusation, laugh it off as absurd and reason with John's logical side—maybe even bribe him into silence with the promise of a whole year's supply of sweet bread.

But the voice was like an echo, intangible and easily suffocated by silence. Her dry eyes wouldn't blink. Her lungs would not inhale. Even the dizzy tingles swirling up her arms and neck and raising her hair were not enough to relax her stiff posture.

John turned and fled.

The cracks of snapping branches and the squelching of mud trailed him for a minute. Then silence cloaked the forest once more, deeper and blacker than when she had first entered.

Panic clawed up her belly and throat, shattering the ice freezing her lungs. She drank in the cool air, drawing it in with huge, rasping gulps that choked her dry throat. Leaping to her feet, panting, she stumbled over to the smouldering herb bundles, gathering what she could with shaking fingers and smothering the rest in snow to hide the traces of her magic.

She had to beat John home, sneak in without anyone seeing her. If he didn't see her return, if her house looked quiet and undisturbed, maybe he would doubt what he had seen enough to give her a chance at an alibi. It was her only hope.

Taking a deep breath to compose her weak and wobbly limbs, she closed her eyes and unlocked the compartment at the back of her mind, the one that separated the storm cloud from the rest of her brain. She let it billow to the fore, roiling and swelling to every corner, embracing the building tension. Energy crackled through her body, charging through her veins and muscles, reshaping them with stinging, shocking stabs. Her bones lightened. Her arms elongated and her body shrank, toes curling into talons and nose curving into a hooked beak. Feathers fanned out across her skin, rippling in the light breeze.

She opened her eyes to a world with more variation of colours than the one she had closed them on, and examined her wings, flexing the muscles that hadn't been stretched this way in a few years. Her ebony and ivory feathers gleamed with a silver moonlit sheen. With her sharpened hearing, she could make out John's wheezes and heavy footfalls just over half a kilometre away.

Gertrude lifted her wings and flapped into the air, and she careened toward the people she must protect at all costs.

Distant thunder rumbled as she carefully clicked the door shut behind her, grateful she had not been soaked by the rain starting to patter on the roof and drip from the eaves. No light had been on in John's house; she hoped that meant she had arrived home before him. Darkness crowded her senses, pressing in on her, but she dared not light a candle. Sliding her foot out in front of her, she extended her hand, and she crept forward one small step at a time, trusting her memory to guide her toward her room, hoping she would feel obstacles before crashing into them.

"Ma?"

Gertrude startled, heart jumping to her throat and hand flying to her chest.

A dark silhouette shifted in the blackness ahead, short and timid.

"Nonie?" Gertrude whispered, recognizing her younger daughter's voice. "Is that you? What are you doing out of bed?"

"I had a nightmare and woke up to thunder." Even timid and choked with restrained sobs, Nonie's small four-year-old voice carried in the silence of the sleeping house. Gertrude glanced at the shadows shifting in her peripheral vision before reaching out for Nonie's tiny hand and enclosing it gently in her own.

"Oh, my darling," Gertrude breathed. "Come, I'll sing the shadows into light."

She guided Nonie back to her bed, lifting the blankets slowly so as not to disturb Abigail, who slumbered peacefully next to Nonie's empty spot on the bed they shared. Abigail twitched when Nonie pressed her back against her older sister's, but didn't wake up. Perching on the edge of the bed, Gertrude stroked Nonie's hair off her forehead and sang a short, whispered lullaby.

Daughter of darkness, fear not the shadows.
When deep night falls, seek the hallows.

Shadows cloak secrets, just waiting to be found.
In the dark there is light, and treasures abound.

Flashes of light in a dark thunderstorm,
Glowing stars twinkle against black skies.
Silver moonbeams shift a shadow's form,
And summer nights shimmer with fireflies.

Daughter of darkness, for you there is light,
Wherever you go, even in the darkness of night.
Shadows blanket slumber, protect our dreams,
So sleep, and remember, the dark is not what it seems.

Gertrude planted a soft kiss just above Nonie's closed eyes and backed out of the room without creaking the floorboards once. She paused in the doorway of her own room, across from her children's, peering at the curled lump in the bed that was her husband, to ensure he slept soundly. She exhaled a sigh of relief at the rhythmic rise and fall of Abner's chest beneath the blanket.

Her heavy heart ached in her chest, cradled in a cot of nostalgia and guilt. She loved being able to share Armindish traditions, like the lullaby, with her children, but not being able to let go of her past was what had led to her discovery tonight. What had she been thinking? The time hadn't been right. It was still too soon after the hangings. Nothing had really changed. Maybe nothing ever would change. Hatred and fear of the unknown did not dissipate with the changing of seasons. Acceptance did not follow persecution.

She knew these truths, but the temptation to ignore them had been too strong. Denying her magic, denying herself for so long, had taken its toll. Living with constant fear had eroded her walls and weakened her resolve.

She would not let her family pay for her moment of weakness.

Should we all flee tonight?

Though she longed to shake Abner awake, to gather their meagre possessions and leave Salem under cover of darkness, she knew Abner would never comply. His whole life was in Salem: his reputable apothecary business, his family and friends. And he didn't know she could do magic, that she had walked through a portal from another world. She had never shared that part of herself with him. Though his love for her ran deep, Gertrude didn't think he would believe her even if she confessed now. He didn't believe in witchcraft, had always thought the accusations and hangings absurd, and if she showed him, he might not think her a witch—but he may think her brain addled.

The promise of death was nothing to the heartbreak of her husband looking at her like a stranger, a dangerous madwoman capable of hurting him or her children. Unreachable. Untouchable.

A life without her children and husband would be excruciating, but a life where they didn't recognize her or fell out of love with her would be unendurable torture.

In the darkness of her room, aided by the flashes of lightning between rumbles of thunder, Gertrude opened the wooden box that contained her favourite quill, and pried open the tiny groove at the bottom, revealing a secret compartment. She plucked out the minuscule vial nestled inside and tucked it in a tiny pocket she had sewn onto the inside of her shift.

If death knocked on her door, she would greet it on her own terms.

She didn't have to wait long. Rain pelted the roof in a steady stream through the pewter fog of dawn a few days later, and Gertrude had just handed Abigail a small bowl of cornmeal mush with milk when death pounded on the door, rattling the lock. Abigail jumped, and her spoon slid from the bowl to clatter on the floor.

"What on earth?" Abner put down the letter he had been poring over at the table to frown at the door. "Who could be here at this hour?"

"Maybe someone needs an urgent remedy," Gertrude suggested, trying to ignore her rapid heartbeat and the lump swelling in her throat.

The pounding shook the door frame this time.

Heaving himself out of the chair, Abner sighed and rubbed his eyes. As he crossed to the door, he muttered, "But I've only broken my fast with one bite."

"Bad news, I'm afraid, Abner," Constable Herrick said when Abner opened the door. "I have a warrant here for your wife's arrest."

Her husband glanced from the men behind the constable to Gertrude with bemusement, one corner of his lips curled up in expectant mirth as he waited for the joke. Gertrude fixed her gaze on a point over the constable's shoulder, neither defiant nor intimidated, though her pulse jumped in her neck.

"Gertrude Browne, you have been accused of witchcraft and will face an examination and trial," said Constable Herrick with a grimace. Every line of his face sagged with weary resignation.

"*Witchcraft?*" Abner repeated, aghast. "You can't be serious."

"What's witchcraft?" Nonie asked around a mouthful of bread.

"Something bad people do," said Abigail faintly, worry creasing her brow as she looked between the men and her mother.

"Ma's not bad!" exclaimed Nonie indignantly.

"Of course she's not," agreed Abner, and the defence of her character came so easily, so naturally, as though the idea of evil existing in his wife was ludicrous, that she almost closed the gap between them and kissed him.

The constable's voice became gentler as he added, "Look, Abner, it's most likely just temporary. Things are changing. But under the circumstances, we must go through the procedure."

"What circumstances?"

"John Hodge claims he saw Gertrude in the woods two nights ago. He says he saw her summoning the devil and making leaves... dance."

Gertrude noticed Constable Herrick avoided meeting her eyes, and heat crept up her cheeks, embarrassed guilt and anger mingling in her blood and setting it to boil.

"What proof has he?" she challenged.

Constable Herrick sighed, rubbing the back of his neck. "Well, that's just it. John took us out to the spot in the woods where he saw you, and while we didn't find any signs of the devil being summoned, we did find this."

He gestured to one of the men behind him, who held out a white handkerchief. Unremarkable from any other handkerchief in the village, except for one small detail. Tucked between the folds of the corner seam, in bright, brazen red thread, the letters G.B. had been stitched.

Gertrude Browne.

A bold statement she had dared to make, stitching her initials in such an immodest colour. An act of defiance against having to adjust to the belittlement and dehumanization of women in this world that she hadn't been used to.

Now a suicide letter written in her own blood.

"That's ridiculous. Just because it has her initials on it?" scoffed Abner. "Even if it were hers, it has nothing to do with witchcraft."

"There was also this, on the ground beside the handkerchief," Constable Herrick said softly into the silence, for even her daughters had been hushed by the sight of their mother's handkerchief. He reached into his pocket and held something small and round aloft between his pointer finger and thumb. Something that glowed with its own silver-white light. Something that contained a pearlescent mist that swirled and twisted with independent, unnatural movement.

Her moonstone.

Gertrude had been so worried, so desperate to avoid anything to do with magic, that she hadn't touched her pouch since that night. She hadn't noticed the stone had gone missing.

Churning and bubbling like a potion in a cauldron, her stomach clenched against a wave of nausea, but she pushed it down, keeping her face blank. Even with the handkerchief and the moonstone, they had no solid evidence, nothing to prove that it wasn't all John's imagination or the byproduct of a vengeful vendetta.

But when she noticed the tears brimming in her children's eyes and the quiver of their chins, she knew it didn't matter if the evidence was weak or contrived. A score of innocents had already paid the price of blind hatred and fear. She would walk barefoot through the burning lava in the pits beneath Vasmorloth before she would make the mistake of placing hope in justice. Nothing was more important than protecting her daughters.

Abner opened his mouth to argue again, but Gertrude cleared her throat pointedly to cut him off.

"It's fine. I'll go," she said, stepping forward. She would not be dragged away and have her daughters fear for their mother. She would walk out with her head held high. "Don't spoil the children's breakfast over a silly misunderstanding, Abner. You must think of them. Like the constable said, it's just temporary."

As she passed her daughters, she paused and knelt before them. She refused to make promises she couldn't keep or offer the comfort of her return. If these were to be her last words to her children, she didn't want them to be empty platitudes and broken promises for them to begrudge later. But she could offer them love.

"Now you be brave while Mommy is away. Be good for Daddy, and be good to each other. I don't know what tomorrow will bring, but there is nothing to fear in the unknown. All darkness has light, remember? You just need to find it. If you get lost, hold aloft the torch of my love for you, right here." She pressed a palm to each of their chests, over their hearts. "It will burn there brightly, always."

She planted a kiss on each of their foreheads, then turned to her husband. She dared not kiss him in front of the constable and other men—she was in enough trouble without adding impropriety to the list—but she met his wide, watering hickory eyes and poured her love for him, for the life they had created and shared together, into the intensity of her gaze.

"Be steadfast, my love," she whispered. "There's nothing to mourn. All will be fine."

Then she turned and walked out the door with her head held high, grateful for the raindrops sliding down her face, masking her silent tears.

Had it only been a month since she had stolen away in the night, her spirit unencumbered and wild, reflecting on how she had managed to retain happiness despite all the sacrifices she had made? And now here she huddled, freezing and miserable on the hard stone floor of her cell, shackled to the wall with an iron cuff digging into her wrist and hunger gnawing at her belly.

The constable's words still reverberated in her mind like the drum roll of execution.

You will go to trial.

You will go to trial.

You will go to trial.

The time had come for another sacrifice.

Right now, she was still innocent. She had been accused of witchcraft, but no verdict had been reached, no sentence given. The only legacy she would pass down to her children would be an accusation, one that would hopefully be proved false in time. But if they pronounced her a witch? That brand would never fade. Even if they left her children alone and never accused them of inheriting their mother's witchcraft, her daughters would always be painted with the same brush, branded wicked and unworthy among their peers because of their mother. Their prospects, their future, would be forever altered.

She wasn't willing to risk their happiness for hers. Justice had forsaken these parts, stealing hope away with it.

With shaking, white fingers, she slowly pulled out the tiny vial from her hidden shift pocket. She uncorked it, then tilted her head back and emptied the pale lavender liquid into her mouth, swilling the contents across her tongue before swallowing.

Pinpricks of blackness winked at the edges of her vision. Blood rushed in her ears like a storm-swollen river, and her lungs flattened as though compressed by heavy stones. She just managed to tuck the empty vial back into her shift pocket before she slumped sideways, her head smacking the stone floor—and she knew no more.

Gertrude woke to a deeper and denser darkness than she had ever known, and for a moment she feared the elixir had been too strong and had let her cross over the line to death instead of keeping her hovering on the side of barely alive. She couldn't feel her heart beating.

Then...

Whump.

A frail thrum, barely perceptible, but there. Then, thirty seconds later...

Whump.

At first the beats were slow and distant, an expired heart's echoes, but they soon quickened and strengthened, pounding in time with rapid pounding above her. Pounding that vibrated and shook the darkness around her. Pounding that showered her face in dust, forcing her to close her eyes. Pounding so close it rattled her brain and stabbed her ears.

A pounding like a nail being hammered into wood.

Gertrude's breathing caught up with her rapid heartbeat as she slowly reached up and touched rough, splintered wood less than half a metre above her head.

A coffin.

Panic gripped her chest and squeezed her shoulders, pinching and pressing until she couldn't breathe. She closed her eyes and seized the magic in her flickering core, drawing on the comfort of its warmth to stop herself from flinging off the coffin lid.

You did this on purpose. The coffin is part of the plan. Don't panic. Don't scream.

Breathe. Breathe. Breathe.

She repeated this mantra in her head over and over, until her heart and breaths slowed. Unsure how to create more oxygen with Air magic, she poked a dozen small, discreet holes in the wood with tiny, concentrated blasts of air upon each hammer of another nail, letting in dots of daylight like stars winking into existence in the night sky. Then she waited, focusing only on breathing through her nose and listening to the scraping and crunching of final adjustments to her grave.

News of her death must have reached her family by now. Maybe even a service had been held. She wasn't sure what allowances they would grant her family if she had been accused but had never gone to trial, and she also wasn't sure how long the elixir had lasted. Its potency had been an estimate, since she had never tried to slow her heartbeat to near death before.

Was her husband crying? Were her children distraught? She hoped her innocence in the absence of conviction brought them some small comfort. Dying of illness in prison was better than dying by the noose in a public execution. Hopefully, folk would take pity on her family and aid them instead of avoiding them like the plague. They at least appeared to be giving her a proper burial.

The sprays of shovelled dirt finally ceased an hour later as dusk darkened her air holes, and Gertrude felt her coffin being lifted into the air. Grunts huffed above her, and boots shuffled across the rocky dirt as they lowered her coffin into the hole they had dug. They set it down gently, then clambered back from the hole, panting.

This was it. Her chance to escape without suspicion before they buried her alive.

She plucked a strand of magic from her tangled core and swung it out like a battering ram toward the forest she knew bordered the graveyard on one side, knocking a tree crashing to the ground.

"What the devil was that?" yelped one of the gravediggers.

Gertrude flung another strand at the trees.

"Fire!" screamed another gravedigger. "I told you these woods were haunted!"

"Don't be such a coward. I'm sure there's an explanation," said a third, with a heavy sigh that sounded more put out than scared. "Come on, let's go check it out."

Footsteps thundered away from her grave, and Gertrude held her breath, straining her ears. Veins throbbed in her neck, and she unstuck her gummed lips, trying to clear her dry throat.

Silence, save the crackling of flames.

Gertrude popped every nail holding down the coffin lid with magic and slid it to the side, careful not to inflict damage. Glancing around to make sure no one watched, she wobbled out on shaky legs, replaced the lid, and transformed into a lightning bird.

Wings spread wide, she leapt into the air and flew to the treetops to perch on a branch that concealed her while allowing her to watch the graveyard. Only once the fire had been doused and the gravediggers had returned to shovel dirt onto her coffin did she turn her back on Salem and fly away. She left behind her heart and took only her hollowed, harrowed soul.

One

77 Years Later, Keleb-Sola, Carmelle, Arwé

Gliding past the jagged peak's craggy shoulder, Arínor tilted her ebony wings, turning to loop around the pointed tip before diving down the cliffside. Wind shrieked in her ears and flattened the downy feathers framing her sharp eyes, and thunder clapped in her wake like a sparkwheel of Éaloth. She extended her wings and banked right mid-dive to speed around the mountaintop in tight, upward circles until she reached the peak again, then dived down the other side of Vellé. Halfway down, she unfolded her wings and halted abruptly, turning to look up at the peak. A thick bruised-pewter-and-purple storm cloud billowed above the peak, lightning crackling along its underbelly.

Raw, untamed power on display, a power *she* had created. A reminder that she possessed the power to protect her roots, to be the anchor in an otherwise unmoored existence. She had needed that reminder after the unsettling events of yesterday had left her feeling adrift again.

Arínor clicked her beak in satisfaction and turned to swoop toward the grassy hillside of the mountain's arms. After angling her wings to slow herself down, she hovered a metre or two off the ground for a wingbeat before shape-shifting back into her human form in mid-air and landing on her feet in a crouched position, fist anchoring her to the ground. Frost clung to the grass and laced the wild plants like a glittering spiderweb. She breathed deeply, letting the earthy scent of dewy moss and rich soil calm her racing heart and heaving chest. Exhilaration tingled in every nerve of her body, the thrill of the flight coursing through her.

Flying in her lightning bird form was the epitome of freedom, of a life unburdened by expectation or the weight of regret. If she didn't also crave the comfort of companionship and belonging, she would stay a lightning bird longer than stints of a few sprinkled, sporadic hours.

A cool, crisp wind lifted her tangled black hair off her sweat-slicked neck and caressed her hot cheeks. The breeze tickled her bare arms and raised the hairs on her pale, milky skin. She uncurled her crouched body and straightened, hand shielding her eyes from the weak rays of early-morning sun slanting through the patches of grey clouds quilting the sky.

Below her the valley of Keleb-Sola lay pocketed between towering Harth and Vellé, the two tallest peaks in central Carmelle. The pointy, lopsided, steep-gabled roofs of the Armindish village houses poked up between densely packed trees, some bare, the leaves already wilted and fallen, others still bursting with sprays of vermilion and ruby. Arínor loved this time of year, when the valley walked the leaf-strewn path between life and death in its usual mid-autumn mingling of dichotomies.

At the end of the village nearest her, a vast lake glittered. Wagons littered the landscape on the outskirts of the village, and a few houses dotted the bare hillsides of the mountains' lower slopes, including Arínor's. Drawn to the familiar black and grey stones of their crooked chimney, Arínor spotted her family's scarlet-and-sapphire wagon trundling over the rugged, rolling hills bordering their house.

Stomach fluttering like moth wings, she snatched her birch basket full of the herbs she had gathered before her flight, tucked the handle in the crook of her elbow, and ran down the hill, hair streaming behind her like the trailing black smudge of a running bragûl. Her sister and mother would be home soon, back from their trek to Vrena village, between Lenia and Dharmaelia, and she wanted to be home to greet them.

The earthy, slightly minty scent of lauré herbs greeted Arínor when she opened the door to her empty cottage. She glanced at the small cauldron simmering above a single flame on the long stone potion ledge jutting out from the opposite wall, steam rising in curls from its bubbling, murky surface. Glass clinked and something clattered, followed by an indignant squawk from a shelf above the ledge.

"Stop stealing ingredients, Ruse," admonished Arínor without looking in her pet magpie's direction.

Ruse flapped down to the ledge by the cauldron, chattering in his raspy trill at Arínor as she set her basket down and started sorting the herbs she had gathered. Long, reedy yíxa herbs in one pile, short, flowered xana herbs in another. When Arínor did not commiserate with his chattering complaints, Ruse begrudgingly plucked a xana out of the basket with his beak and dropped it on the pile.

"It's about time you made yourself useful," muttered Arínor, but she stroked his white chest feathers absently, continuing to sort with one hand.

"You spoil that bird too much," chided a voice behind her. Arínor looked over her shoulder to see Gertie, an elder Armindí who had been serving Arínor's family business for decades, bustling into the cottage, patterned apron cradling her own collection of treasures. "He's much too dependent on you, both for the food you allow him to sneak and the affection. What will he do if he must survive in the wild again?"

"Why would he have to?" countered Arínor. "I'm not planning on going anywhere."

"No one *plans* to abandon the known for the unknown, yet it happens all the same. It's called life, dear. Or death, for that matter," Gertie added, joining Arínor. She tipped the contents of her apron onto the ledge on the other side of the cauldron, spilling an assortment of herbs, fungi, and the autumnal flower veryl into an unorganized jumble.

"Well then, Ruse will just have to adjust if his world changes from the known to the unknown along with mine," said Arínor, pulling jars down from a different shelf from the one Ruse had been ransacking. "He's probably more adaptable than me."

"Everyone's more adaptable than you."

Arínor paused mid-twist of a jar lid, frowning at Gertie. She watched her swipe her wiry charcoal-grey hair out of her sandy-brown eyes with the back of her hand and select one of the veryl flowers, which she dropped into the cauldron. The bubbling contents turned a violent shade of vermilion, and a frothy foam expanded across the surface. With the pointed fingernail of her thumb, she sliced a thin layer of the fugos mushroom and tossed it into the mix. The foam thinned and evaporated, leaving the surface smooth and rippling once more. With a satisfied nod, Gertie stirred the elixir, either unaware she had uttered an insult or indifferent to Arínor's feelings.

Did everyone view Arínor that way? Lacking a fundamental trait of being an Armindí?

"You don't think I'm adaptable?" asked Arínor, careful not to let her voice waver.

"For a mortal, maybe, but for an Armindí living an untethered existence, always ready to march down whatever new path life lays before her feet? You may embrace adventure and value freedom, but you have always clung to your roots, to the familiar."

Arínor pressed her fingertips lightly against the ledge, vision swirling as though she had stood up too fast. Keeping her tone as neutral as possible, trying to withhold whining from her voice, she said, "I don't think that's quite fair. I have always embraced the Armindish ways, travelling across Carmelle in a nomadic lifestyle, living in the moment instead of for a fate or destiny, trusting that I will still find safe footing on the non-linear path."

"When was the last time you went on a trek?" Gertie countered.

"Last summer."

"Without your family," Gertie clarified.

"I... well, I..." Arínor floundered, gaping at Gertie, blood draining from her face to throb in her ears. She hadn't been on a trek without family since her disastrous, traumatizing initiation trek fifteen years ago, and Gertie knew perfectly well why. How could she use the worst moment of her life against her like that? Hurt coiled around her core, curling in on itself like a wounded dragon, and she cast her watery eyes back down to the yíxa she had been adding to the jar.

Gertie's rough hand rested atop Arínor's, and she said soothingly, "I don't mean to upset you, Nor. There's nothing wrong with loving your family and wanting the comfort of their presence. Just be careful not to let your roots dig too deep, or you'll never survive when life inevitably dislodges and exposes them."

After a moment, Arínor nodded and squeezed Gertie's fingers. Though she wasn't family by blood, Arínor knew her advice stemmed from concern, not criticism. But when she opened her mouth to tell Gertie as much, she noticed her friend's wince.

"Oh, Gertie, I'm so sorry!" cried Arínor, releasing her fingers at once.

"Don't apologize for showing affection. It's not your fault I have stiff, brittle bones from centuries of shape-shifting. You may suffer from the same affliction one day. These frosty autumn mornings don't help. Pass me that salve over there."

Arínor grabbed a shallow, circular tin behind the cauldron, twisted the lid open, inhaling the strong, cool mint scent, and handed it to Gertie. With each rub of the salve into her clicking joints, Gertie emitted a moaning sigh. Arínor didn't try to hide the concern she could feel puckering her brow. "Here, let me help you," she offered, reaching for the tin.

"I'd rather you call on the stars to enhance the potency of the starflowers in this salve and increase the healing power," said Gertie with a cheeky grin, flashing her crooked, crowded teeth.

Arínor scowled. "Ma wouldn't approve, and she'll be home any minute."

"She just doesn't want to see you get hurt. Fear of Celestial magic grows every day, and we've all seen how unforgiving people can be when blinded by their fear of the unknown."

Arínor couldn't suppress a shudder this time, eyes stinging with unshed tears as though she had been slapped. "Did you swallow a dose of truth serum this morning? Or do you just enjoy wielding painful memories and harsh truths like a double-bladed axe?"

"Well, age *does* lend itself to speaking uncomfortable truths with blunt, unflinching force, but I don't aim to wound on purpose. I worry about you, Arínor," Gertie admitted, returning to her potion. "In our line of work, you witness a lot of trauma and face realities most try to avoid or guard against. Ninaya knows I have seen more than most how others' fear can be so consuming it forever alters the course of your own life. You can't control someone else's fear. The Armindí know this. We have faced fear from outsiders our whole lives, from those who don't understand our ways or abilities or evolution from lightning birds. We learned long ago that if you try to control the uncontrollable, you will lose everything, even yourself."

"I won't lose myself, Gertie," Arínor assured her, annoyance pricking her tense shoulders. She picked up a stone pestle and began crushing the xana she had collected beneath it, releasing a cloyingly sweet aroma. "Ma isn't demanding too great a sacrifice by asking me to refrain from using Celestial magic for a while, until things in Carmelle settle down."

"No? I guess the rumours in the village of a certain Miss Stella receiving a... *lunar* gift must have been false, then," replied Gertie, her eyes sparkling with sly mischief.

Arínor shot her a sharp look, flutters swooping low in her stomach at her lover's name. "That's different. I didn't just enchant that bottle yesterday. It—"

"You don't need to explain to me, but I think my point still stands. I was young and naive like you once too, sure I knew how to balance sacrifice and happiness. I was wrong, and I paid the price. I don't want that for you. If you make the wrong sacrifice, you may regret it forever."

Though the xana had been ground into a fine powder already, Arínor continued to twist and stamp the pestle, stalling her response. The low rumble of a trundling wagon drifted through the open window, and Arínor dropped the pestle.

"That must be them. They're home!"

"How convenient," mumbled Gertie as Arínor streaked past her, startling Ruse as she ran out the door.

Her chest swelled at the sight of the colourful painted wooden wagon bobbing into view over the crest of the hill, its ruby and sapphire patterns igniting the comforting flame of home in her heart. The wagon had been her walls, her sanctuary, her escape. Her shelter from the world's cruelty, her ticket to freedom and adventure. Witness to the greatest loves and losses of her life.

But nothing would ever feel more like home than the people clambering out of the wagon. Her sister, Arietté, came first, lowering the wooden steps and bending at an awkward angle to fit through the door with her daughter, Anya, on one hip and the guiding hand of her husband, Menkus, on the other. Before she had descended two steps, her twin boys pushed past her, catapulting down the steps and into Arínor's waiting arms.

"Auntie Nor!" they squealed, knocking the wind out of her as they wrapped their arms around her middle and squeezed.

"Élí, Kat, I missed you!" Arínor wheezed. "How was Vrena?"

"Boring," moaned Kat, releasing her.

"Was not. You're just upset because Ma wouldn't let you jump off that cliff," said Élí.

Arínor gaped at Kat, eyes wide and mouth open in horror. "You tried to jump off a *cliff*?"

"I wasn't trying to *jump* off it. I was trying to *fly* off it, like Auntie Nor," whined Kat.

Her breath vacated her lungs, and bumps pimpled her arms. Had she almost been responsible for her nephew's death by just being herself?

"Don't look so horrified, Arínor. My son's reckless behaviour is not your fault," said Aríetté, joining them. "He knows he cannot shape-shift into a lightning bird, and throwing himself off a cliff won't change that."

"You don't know that!" protested Kat. "What if my body just needs the proper motivation to transform?"

Aríetté threw up her hands in exasperation, and Menkus rolled his eyes behind her.

"Sorry, Kat, but your ma's right," said Arínor, bending low with her hands on her knees to look her nephew in the eyes. "We've talked about this before. You're seven. If you could shape-shift, you would probably know by now. Do you feel a storm cloud brewing in your mind? Sharp pain in your bones or muscles? Have you ever woken up with black feathers clinging to your skin?"

Slowly Kat shook his head and scuffed his boot across the pebbled path to their cottage.

"You know what you can do that I can't, though?" Arínor asked rhetorically. "That camouflage curse. I bet you're even better at it now than before you left on the trek."

"I am!" exclaimed Kat, brightening.

"Excellent! Well then, why don't you go practise on that stump over there while I help your ma and grandma unload? And then you can show me."

Kat rushed off with Élí.

"I'll go mitigate the inevitable arguments," volunteered Menkus, squeezing his wife's shoulder and following the twins.

"And how's Miss Anya doing?" Arínor asked her two-year-old niece.

"Struggling," Aríetté admitted, pulling her toddler's thumb out of her mouth. "She got sick on the road home and hasn't slept properly for two days."

"And neither have you," Arínor guessed, surveying her sister's tousled straw-coloured hair poking out from beneath her light blue headscarf, heavy lids, and purple shadows ringed under her eyes. She reached out for her niece to transfer her to her own hip, and Aríetté knuckled her back, stretching.

"Thanks," said Aríetté. "It's fine. I'm fine. At least the fever has broken now. Winter's chill is upon us, but it has not yet deepened to the cold that pierces through blankets and seeps into bones. We left before that point, not wanting to take the risk with the children. Maybe we should have stayed, though... The coin's not much."

Aríetté reached into her skirt pocket and pulled out an indigo velvet purse, shaking it a little. A few coins clinked together, more faintly than Arínor had expected, and it looked only a quarter full. Arínor's cheeks sagged, and she closed her eyes against a wave of weariness. Anya reached over her shoulder for her brothers, and Arínor put her down. She watched her waddle over to the stump where Kat sat with his eyes screwed tight in concentration.

"It's a tough time of year," said Gertie from behind Arínor, coming to join them. "Everyone's preparing for winter, and there's not a lot of coin to spare, or goods to trade."

"We did get a good amount of food and supplies in trade," Aríetté said, gesturing at the wagon. "Qir'a grain, nuts for grinding into flour and paste, tolo beans, some root vegetables. It should be enough to help us through the winter."

"Should?" echoed Arínor.

"Oh, and I suppose you would have let the pregnant woman in Vrena suffering from extreme vomiting rupture her throat or die from dehydration because she couldn't pay for the concoction to slow it down?" said Aríetté, red rising beneath her freckled cheeks. "Or you would have forced the melancholy woman in Runoxa with no support and no coin, distraught at just finding out she was with child, to deal with things herself in a dangerous way instead of providing her with the herbal tea that would terminate it in the early stages safely?"

"Of course not! I wasn't suggesting you shouldn't have helped the women who needed it!" Arínor exclaimed indignantly. "I'm not a monster. I was just concerned—"

"Sometimes we have to sacrifice our own comfort for the women who have already suffered so many sacrifices," Aríetté interjected.

"Easy there, Aríetté. Climb down from the moral high ground before you topple off," said Gertie. "Arínor is just being practical. Frankly, if it weren't for Arínor's practicality, we all would have starved long ago. You have your father's idealism Aríetté, but idealism alone won't feed your children. Exchanging sacrifices isn't always a lucrative currency."

"Sorry," said Aríetté, pinching her nose and rubbing her eyes. "I didn't mean to snap at you, Arínor. I'm just tired. And I wouldn't let my kids starve." She gave Gertie a dark scowl, her grey eyes like thunderclouds threatening rain.

"Where's Ma?" Arínor asked hastily, changing the subject.

Aríetté shrugged. "Forging a new path to the latrine with the force of her fury."

At Gertie's and Arínor's confused expressions, Aríetté beckoned them to the other side of the wagon, where they had a clear view of their mother, Lís, trampling the long grass with her pacing stomps.

"Is there a particular reason she's in such a good mood?" asked Arínor sarcastically.

"Probably something to do with our stop in the village on the way home," replied her sister. "Ma stopped in at the apothecary to sell them the remedies and elixirs we hadn't sold on our trek, and when she came back out, she was red in the face and practically steaming from the ears. When I asked her about it, she just said that Ulfor had told her a very disturbing story."

Arínor's heart plummeted. One of the biggest gossips in Keleb-Sola, Ulfor also happened to be her lover Stella's aunt. "I better go talk to her."

Her mother did not glance up from her pacing, not even when Arínor perched on a boulder a few feet away and drew her legs up to her chest, tucking her long, pleated black skirt around her ankles and leaning her chin against her knees.

"I'm waiting, Arínor," said Lís, turning on her heel and pacing away from her daughter.

"For what?"

"For you to deny it! To tell me it's not true, that Ulfor is just being a spiteful old woman determined to ruin the happiness of young lovers because she's alone and always will be."

"Well, I do think that part's true," muttered Arínor.

"But you can't deny that her story is true. You can't tell me that her claim of you giving Stella a bottle with a miniature moon suspended inside that gives off actual moonlight is a lie."

Arínor pressed her closed lips into her knees, confirming the rumour with her silence.

For a long moment, her mother echoed her silence, staring at the storm clouds still roiling above Vellé, as though searching for the right words. Her pacing ceased, and she plopped down on the ground in front of Arínor's rock, facing her daughter.

"Outsiders have feared the Armindí for centuries not because they don't know anything about us," Lís began, "but because they only know partial truths. They know we evolved from lightning birds and some of us can still shape-shift into one, but they don't know how rare that is becoming. They know lightning birds can create storms, but they don't know *why* we would create one, or where, and fear we will ruin their crops and endanger their loved ones. They know we harness Elemental magic in a different way, and they might even know that way is through curses and our affinity with potions and elixirs. But they don't know the intention behind the elixirs and curses, if we always use them for good or if they're more sinister. And when people only know half-truths, they tend to assume the worst about the half they don't know."

Arínor nodded, understanding where her mother was going with this speech. "It's the same with Celestial magic. I get it, Ma. I do. I may not always make the best decisions, but I'm thirty-four. I'm not a child. I know the average person's knowledge of Celestial magic comes from the horrific stories they hear of Vashi using it, and its rarity among Carmellians means a lack of opportunity to study it or establish a set of rules or predictable patterns, like with Elemental magic. I know better than most that even the half-truths are exaggerated and misinformed, so how could anyone be expected to reach a positive conclusion for the unknown halves? I would be skeptical too. I still *am* skeptical. I can wield Celestial magic, but the half-truths I know are wildly speculative, unpredictable, and incomplete."

"Then maybe you shouldn't wield it, at least for now," her ma said. Her quick, confident words belied her gentle voice.

Arínor raked her hand through her hair, shaking her head. "By nature, Celestial magic is not all darkness. The blackness of the void is countered by the bright light of the sun and stars, or the more subtle, complex refracted light of the moon. I know there's risk when so much is still hidden to me, but imagine what's left to discover. Imagine the possibilities when fearmongering does not suppress the nonconformities of innovation."

"But doesn't it demand sacrifice?" whispered Lís, her voice cracking and quivering.

"*Life* demands sacrifice, Ma, not just Celestial magic. Isn't that what you have taught me since I was a child? Life is a balance of sacrifice and reward, of regret and contentment, of loss and love. We sacrifice comfort, reputation, and respect to help women in need make one less sacrifice of their own, to know we made a difference in someone's life. Why should Celestial magic be any different? What I use Celestial magic for doesn't require sacrifice of life. I can't say for sure if Vashi's use of it does or if that's more misinformation, but imagine if all Armindí were judged by one Armindí's malicious curse. Would that be fair?"

"Of course not, but it happens, Arínor. Whether they should or not, people paint in broad strokes, and if there's paint outside the lines, they want to fix it. Enough of Carmelle thinks Celestial magic is too far outside the lines, and the way to fix it is to wipe it off the canvas. That kind of thinking is so dangerous—"

"I *know*, Ma," Arínor interjected, her raw voice breaking. She curled her fingers into the flesh of her crossed arms, digging her nails in until they drew half-moon lines of blood. Her mother knew better than to mention her old partner's name, but the allusion to that night fifteen years ago still hung in the air between them, in the void of unspoken words. The night she would regret for the rest of her life.

"I'm sorry, Arínor. I don't mean to upset you. I know you are aware of the dangers associated with Celestial magic more than anyone," her ma said. "It's just... things are worse now. Even the Armindí are starting to fear Vashi, and it's harder to know friend from foe. I just want you to be careful, and to consider every decision regarding Celestial magic carefully."

Unshed tears crowded the corners of her eyes and blurred her vision, but Arínor blinked them back. Not trusting the steadiness of her voice, she bit her lip and nodded.

Rolling to the side, Lís groaned as she pushed herself to her feet. "Next time I try to sit cross-legged right after I exit the wagon from a long journey, remind me that my legs will not thank me." She wobbled as she leaned over to hug Arínor and kiss her forehead. "I love you, danukra."

Arínor managed a weak smile at her ma's old term of endearment for her. Daughter of storms. Chaos did brew in her wake, but chaos held beauty too, and possibility. Celestial magic was part of her, like her eyes, or her nose, or her tongue. She could live without it, but she would feel incomplete, stuck in a world of shadows and echoes, hollow as the Void magic she specialized in.

She watched her nephews double over in fits of giggles at the sight of Kat's leg camouflaged against Élí's so it looked as though they shared only three legs between them.

In that moment, she knew she must sacrifice the sense of contentment and wholeness using Celestial magic brought her for the happiness of her family.

Or at least, if she used Celestial magic again, she must not get caught.

Two

"Arínor, wake up!"

The void of her dreamless sleep winked with whispering stars. Arínor stirred, flinging her arm over her face.

"Please, Arínor! It's urgent!"

She bolted upright, whipping her head toward her window, her braid smacking her cheek.

Violet eyes gleamed at her in the darkness.

Arínor reached for her magic, but light flared and illuminated the familiar pointed nose and heart-shaped face to which the violet eyes belonged.

"Curses, Kerena, what under Vasmorloth are you doing sneaking to my window like that?" cried Arínor in a whisper, careful not to let her voice carry lest she wake Anya.

"I'm sorry. I didn't know what else to do. I didn't want to wake the kids by banging on the front door," whispered Kerena, shrinking the sphere of sunlight undulating above her palm to dim the brightness. "But I need your help, Arínor. *We* need your help. Tessa's in so much pain. The midwife is with her, but I thought if you could bring something for the pain, take the edge off, then maybe the midwife could examine her better, or—"

"I'm coming," Arínor assured her friend, already out of bed and shimmying the black skirt from yesterday over her shift. She grabbed a loose black blouse from the floor and shoved her head and arms through the holes, slipped her boots on, leaving the laces undone, and crept across the wooden floorboards, stepping lightly in the spots her practised feet knew didn't creak.

After snatching her black velvet pouch embroidered with feathers from the small desk at the foot of her bed, she turned back to the window, then paused. This was not the first time she'd been called out in the middle of the night, and she kept her pouch stocked and ready with essential potions, teas, salves, and supplies for poultices. But if Kerena's eight-month-pregnant younger sister was in that much pain...

Arínor grabbed a few more ingredients and a little bottle of ruby elixir from a cupboard above her desk, shoved them in her pouch, tightened the drawstring, and tiptoed back over to the bed. She set one foot on the mattress, then paused to listen, peeking over her shoulder at the door to her tiny room.

No footsteps shuffled outside the door. No floorboards creaked or groaned. The low rumbles of her ma's snores drifted faintly through the door's cracks, but she could hear no other sound from within the cottage.

Timing her movements with her ma's snores, she heaved herself through the low window and into the night.

When Kerena burst through the front door of Tessa's cottage, and Arínor hurried on her heels to the rear bedroom, they found Tessa hunched over in bed, arms around her swollen, strained belly in a protective circle. The midwife sat beside her, mopping her sweaty forehead with a cold cloth, one hand rested on Tessa's stomach to monitor the baby's movements.

"How are you, Tess?" Kerena asked, her voice notably breathless from the vigorous pace they had set from Arínor's place. Anxiety slicked her slanted brows with perspiration.

Tessa moaned in response, leaning forward and gripping the blankets in curled fists against the onslaught of another wave of pain. A scream broke through her clenched teeth, raw and ragged, as if her throat had been scraped for hours, and Kerena flinched.

"Hang in there, Tess," Arínor said in a soothing voice, loosening the drawstrings of her pouch and extracting a bag containing the loose ingredients of the special tea she had concocted for pain. "I need hot water," she instructed the room at large.

Kerena had rushed to her sister's side and gripped her hand, squeezing as though she could transfer the pain to herself, so the midwife, Míra, bustled into the kitchen.

By the time Arínor had added one of the extra herbs she had brought to the tea mixture, the one that would counter the potentially harmful effects of the pain-eradicating leaves to make it safe for the baby, Míra was back, bearing a small pot of hot water, a ladle, and an unadorned cup. Her speed could only mean she had heated the water with Fire magic, and not for the first time, Arínor sent a silent thank-you into the void that Míra possessed magic she did not. Most midwives had no magic and relied only on their anatomical and medical knowledge, birthing savvy, and sometimes a talent for herbal remedies and potions, like Arínor's family. Míra's potion skills were unexceptional, which was why she called on Arínor's family more than any other midwife in Keleb-Sola for assistance, but her knowledge and skills were unmatched.

Arínor pinched the tea ingredients between her fingers, then sprinkled them into the pot of hot water and closed the lid, letting them steep.

Tessa screamed again, and her chest heaved as she panted, unable to catch her breath.

"How is she really?" Arínor asked Míra, turning her back on Kerena to shield her from the conversation. "Will she lose the baby?"

"I don't think so," Míra whispered back. "The pain is real and concerning, but she is also panicking, increasing her heartbeats and panting, which makes it worse. It's hard to say for sure when she won't let me examine her. Every time I try, she clenches up and refuses. I think she's scared of what I will discover, terrified of hearing the worst. Remember to breathe, Tessa," Míra instructed over her shoulder as the sound of Tessa's panting ceased for a strangled moment.

"Breathe, Tessa. Breathe," Kerena coached her sister, rubbing her back.

Tessa's gasping exhalation signalled a jolt of relief down Arínor's spine.

"Kerena is terrified too," said Arínor, glancing over her shoulder at her friend. Luckily, she was still focused on her sister and unaware of the whispered conversation. "She has been a wreck this whole pregnancy, hyperattentive to her sister's needs, determined to do everything she can to prevent Tessa from suffering like she did, especially after the last loss."

Míra shook her head grimly, pursing her lips. "Four pregnancies, four miscarriages. I'm still shocked she allowed me to be Tessa's midwife after I failed her the last time."

"Oh, Míra," Arínor whispered, reaching out to squeeze the older woman's hand in gentle solidarity. "It wasn't your fault. Kerena knows that. Sometimes all the sacrifices in the world for the ones we love are not enough. I'm sure you're right and Tessa will be fine. Here, I think the tea is ready."

Arínor opened the lid to ensure the tea had reached the optimal shade of warm hazelnut. Then she used the ladle to hold back the loose herbs and poured some into the cup Míra held.

"Here you are," said Míra to Tessa, careful not to spill the tea as she brought the cup to the bed and tipped it to Tessa's lips. "Drink this, dear. It will help the pain."

Parting her chapped lips, Tessa took small, quivering sips. When the cup had been drained, she rested her head on the pillow Kerena had propped behind her and closed her eyes, breathing deeply through her nose, still working through the pain Arínor knew wouldn't recede for another minute or two.

"Where is Runar?" Arínor asked Tessa, attempting to distract her but also unable to keep a frown from creasing her cheeks. She kept her tone light and neutral, careful not to sound too accusatory as she added, "I thought he was supposed to be back by now."

"He was," said Tessa simply, shifting to unclench her tense muscles as the pain began to ebb.

"He was due back over a week ago," Kerena offered in response to Arínor's narrowed eyes, "but he hasn't returned. A week is not so late when returning from a trek, and he had many heavy instruments to sell and cart around. There are many reasons why he could be delayed."

"I know," said Tessa with a heavy sigh. "And obviously, Tor Stella Lalíté is a huge lake, but Bruthisa, at the southernmost tip, is still about the same distance away as Lenia. So it's not too far, and he'll probably be home any day now."

"I'm sure there's a reasonable explanation," agreed Arínor, but she twisted her skirt in her fingers, trying to ignore her raised arm hair and knotted stomach. The southernmost tip of Tor Stella Lalíté may not be further than Lenia, but it was closer to Vasmorloth, and if the rumours were true, increased activity had been observed along the borders with Vashi's allies.

"Are you ready for me to examine you now?" Míra asked Tessa.

Tessa's eyes flew to her sister's, latching on to her steady gaze like a fingerhold on a cliff.

"I'll be right here by your side," Kerena assured her sister.

Tessa nodded and gritted her teeth. Arínor turned her back, giving them some privacy, and sat on the chair in the far corner of the room, ready to snuggle in night's long arms.

Though her eyes blurred and burned, and her muscles and joints ached, Arínor did not succumb to sleep. Having determined Tessa and the baby were stable but still in danger while Tessa's cramps continued, Míra had initiated a rotation of care: every half hour, Míra would help Tessa change positions to relieve the pressure; every two hours, Arínor supplied her with more tea to regulate her pain and breathing; and Kerena distracted her with continuous back rubs and words of encouragement.

Fiddling with the vial of red liquid she hoped not to have to use, Arínor looked out the open window and watched the stars fade as ebony lightened to charcoal, charcoal to slate.

Could stardust be used as a healing agent in potions?

She had long felt her connection to the stars transcended the boundaries of her Celestial magic, and if she could use her magic to harness stardust, she could mix it in potions to strengthen the solution, the women she helped, and even the babies they carried. Her undulating core pulsed as though eager to conduct the experiment, but she quelled its demands. Though Kerena also had Celestial magic, Arínor noticed her friend did not use it to help her sister, and followed her lead. Perhaps she, too, had become haunted by fear for her loved ones. Arínor could not take risks with Tessa and Míra, not with her ma's warnings still echoing in her head.

When the sky had lightened to a milky silver, Míra examined Tessa again.

"The cramping has dissipated. There is no dilation. The baby is kicking and has not yet lowered. And there is no bleeding," Míra announced. "I am not sure what caused the severe cramping, but they don't appear to have been birthing pains, and I believe both Tessa and her baby are safe for now."

Kerena's palpable relief radiated from her in waves, relaxing her shoulders, deflating her chest as she exhaled held breath, and slouching her rigid spine. Her wide smile reached her bright violet eyes, and Arínor beamed at her friend, her own happiness swelling in her chest.

"I'm so happy you're well, Tessa," said Arínor, the words sticking to her dry tongue a little. She gathered up the few supplies she had taken out of her pouch and cinched the drawstring. "I'll leave you to rest."

"Oh, but you must stay, Arínor. You're exhausted," objected Kerena. "We have a spare cot. Let me set it up for you—"

"No. You and Tessa both need sleep. You'll be in good hands with Míra," said Arínor. "I'll be fine, and I really should be getting back home."

"Well... if you insist..." said Kerena, faltering.

"Thank you so much for coming, Arínor," said Tessa, her eyes brimming with tears of gratitude. "I couldn't have done this without you, truly."

"You know I'm happy to help whenever you need me. Don't hesitate to call if it happens again," said Arínor.

After a last hug for Míra, Arínor stepped out into the beams of pale morning light slicing through the trees bordering Tessa's cottage, like a shimmering nebula billowing between pillars of solidifying stars. She had just reached the edge of the forest and caught a glimpse of fog shrouding the shore of Tor Stella Lalíté when the call of her name halted her feet.

"You forgot this," panted Kerena, hurrying to join her at the edge of a tangled-tree-root path sloping down to the lake. Pinched between her fingers, the vial caught the dawn's glow, lightening the red liquid to pink.

"Thanks," Arínor mumbled, watching Kerena's passive face. She knew it couldn't be easy for her to see this vial again. Arínor had grabbed it on a whim, unsure how she would adapt it for Tessa's needs but knowing she needed an option to try if Tessa's pain became a question of life and death. Kerena's violet eyes had hardened to amethysts, and her mouth had thinned into a straight line, but her chin did not quiver. No tears wet her eyes.

"I'm sorry," Arínor still offered, gesturing at the vial.

"Don't be." Kerena's reply was instant, her stoic voice thick with suppressed emotion.

Arínor's friend didn't elaborate, but she didn't leave either. Her gaze remained fixated on the grey fog rippling over the still, cool blue lake.

"Are you still... content with your decision?" Arínor ventured after a minute, her tone light, casual.

"I don't think 'content' is a word that will ever describe my relationship with that decision," said Kerena slowly, weighing each word—not as though she were trying to choose the right ones but as though uttering them could measure the burden she had been carrying for three years. Measure, but not release. "Nor was it a finite decision. It's one I will have to remake every day for the rest of my life. But I don't regret it."

Kerena turned to face her, a glint of resolution sparking in her amethyst eyes, but also compassion as she seized Arínor's hand in her own. "I can't regret choosing a path that allowed me to finally scramble out of the dark pit I had fallen in, when every other attempt had left me peeled raw and broken. The wounds from four losses are still there—physical and emotional—and I don't know if they will ever fully heal. But I was given the opportunity to free myself before I sank deeper into the pit and was lost forever. Mend the breaks instead of watching them shatter beyond repair. I know I would not have been able to handle the terror and sorrow, the pain and trauma, again. Will I always wonder what might have happened if I had waited and tried one more time to see the baby of my dreams born? Maybe. But it was a risk I no longer had the strength to take. I needed hope, a chance to heal and reclaim my life. I'm grateful you were able to give me that hope."

Arínor pulled Kerena into a hug and said, "I'm grateful to have you as a friend."

Though Arínor knew her mother would be annoyed she had vanished without a word, and would be looking for her to help with the winter-preparation chores, she lingered by the lake after Kerena returned to the cottage, digesting the night's events. Reclining against the bole of a pine, between the thick roots snaking into the water, Arínor fiddled with the moss at her feet. A shard of glass glinted in the sun, its edges smoothed by the shoreline's rocks and sand, its depths clouded. She plucked it out of the moss and rolled it along her palm, lost in thoughts of sacrifice and the unknown.

Kerena had sacrificed the idea of having a child to preserve her sanity, replacing an uncontrollable dream with a more controllable one. Tessa had sacrificed control of body and mind for a promise of uncontrolled, chaotic beauty. Neither path seemed *right* to Arínor, nor did she see those paths as finite. Like Kerena had said, choices had to be made and remade every day. Kerena could change her mind one day, decide she was ready to try for a baby again, and Tessa could change her mind about wanting more. External circumstances could choose a path for them, and then they would have a whole new set of choices to make, new sacrifices to consider for alternative paths to happiness.

It was why the Armindí believed in a non-linear path, a life of adaptability and flexibility, never digging their roots in too deep.

The choice to sacrifice her Celestial magic to protect her family was also one Arínor would have to rechoose every day, but maybe it wasn't as simple as just snuffing it out altogether. Why douse and rebuild a fire when you could reduce it to embers and let it smoulder, stoking it occasionally to release small sparks and keep the fire alive but not burning? Gifting that lunar bottle to Stella had been a lover's foolish mistake, a bold, burning flame destined for discovery.

Arínor glanced around, peering at the still lake and silent tree sentinels. No one was around. No one to witness her magic, with Kerena's cottage the closest dwelling. Could she not stoke the embers to ignite a small spark now?

Concentrating on the piece of glass resting on her palm, she scooped a sliver of light from her core and melded it with a diamond of sunlight sparkling on the lake's surface. She hoped the sun's reflection would be easier to capture, as working with Sun magic was the most difficult aspect of Celestial magic for her. It had the same properties as Star magic, but because her proximity to the sun was much greater, it was stronger and more potent, and it required much more powerful magic. Arínor had always been slightly jealous of Kerena's affinity with Sun magic.

Luckily, her theory proved correct. She trapped the tiny beam of reflected sunlight inside the petal-shaped glass, and on a whim, she embraced the black void behind the light of her core and drew on its depths. Combining its dark matter with the trapped sunlight, she pressed them together, squeezing until they forged a tiny speck of stardust, which breathed life into the glass petal. The murky glass smoothed into a delicate, silken white petal, kissed with sparkling gold at the tip.

"Beautiful," said a voice behind her.

Arínor jumped and dropped the petal, whirling to see Invidia stepping out from behind the bole of a pine a few feet away. Her heart raced, the heat flooding her cheeks as she scrambled to her feet.

"Relax. It's not like I caught you with your skirt up." Invidia laughed, her yellow-tinged emerald eyes glinting with an amusement that matched the one-sided curve of her lips. "You should be proud of your magical creations."

"So… you won't… spread rumours?" Arínor asked, worry injected in her hesitant pauses.

Invidia didn't quite scowl, but she raked her hand through her short strands of tousled ebony hair in exasperation. "Do you really think I would spread rumours about your Celestial magic? Have I ever expressed concern or unease about it?"

"Well... no," admitted Arínor, the heat of her embarrassment fading to an uncomfortable itch. Invidia had only ever shown interest in her Celestial magic, but Arínor wasn't always quite sure what to think of her. She wasn't an Armindí and had just appeared in Keleb-Sola one day after meeting an Armindish family on one of their northern treks, claiming to be a lost soul with no family, who identified with their ways. The Armindí had welcomed her like a long-lost cousin, and Invidia had proven herself a keen, dedicated member of their community. Arínor liked her, and if Invidia unsettled her nerves at times, she tried not to heed it, dismissing the feeling as her own narrow-minded discomfort at not being able to place her within a specific race or geographic region.

"You just can't be too careful these days," she added.

"Ah. Yes, I hear that a lot. In times of uncertainty, when trust becomes the currency, the first ones to feel the sting of people's caution are those who don't truly belong," said Invidia, the barb of bitterness sharpening her tone. "But I guess you know something about that too, or you wouldn't be so concerned about me witnessing your use of Celestial magic."

"Well, maybe us lost souls need to stick together," said Arínor. "Are you in a hurry to be somewhere?"

"I came to check on Tessa. I heard Míra had been summoned, and I was worried," said Invidia, glancing toward the cottage. "Do you know if she's all right?"

"Yes. She's fine," Arínor assured her. "I was with her all night. She's just resting now."

Slumping down against the tree beside where Arínor had been sitting, Invidia rolled her shoulders back and said, "Oh, good. I guess I can sit for a bit, then. I was up late myself—Blaze is sick."

Arínor's eyes must have gone foggier than the clouds blanketing the lake, because Invidia clarified, "Blaze is my horse."

"Right, yes, of course. I'm sorry to hear he's sick," fumbled Arínor. She gave her head a jerky shake as though trying to dislodge a quoxa insect and added, "So you don't fear Celestial magic, then?"

Instead of answering immediately, Invidia picked at the frayed threads of a small hole on the knee of her breeches, almost like a burn hole from a stray spark. After a moment, she said, "Did you know I trained at Nakhana for a time?"

Arínor couldn't stop her lips from parting to match her widened eyes. "Nakhana? The wizard school? I didn't know you had magic."

"Elemental, not Celestial, but yes," replied Invidia, almost apologetically. "I went there to train but didn't stay long. I found their views too narrow, their ideas and rules of acceptable magic too stifling. Even the Illuminators at Nakhana fear what they don't know, but I think some of life's greatest magics and truths can be found in the unknown. Maybe that's why I identify with the Armindí so much. I've never felt I could be bound by the restraints of a linear path. It's a shame societal fears are forcing you to tread a more linear path instead of appreciating the fascinating potential applications of Celestial magic, as I do. That petal... do you mind me asking how you did that? Was it Sun, Star, or Void?"

Arínor raised a brow, impressed by Invidia's knowledge of Celestial magic. "A bit of both Sun and Void. Sun to capture the sunlight's reflection, Void to bring it to life. I know most people think Void magic is all emptiness and deprivation, but I've been experimenting with it, and when combined with other Celestial magics in specific ways, it can create life."

"Fascinating," breathed Invidia, the yellow in her emerald eyes glinting gold. "Giving up something you have such an innate, instinctive gift for, and that is so integral to who you are, seems like too big a sacrifice to make."

"It's not easy," Arínor conceded, "but family, roots, my sense of belonging in this community—they're more integral to my identity, and I can't sacrifice them."

Too late Arínor realized her mistake as Invidia pressed her lips together.

"I'm so sorry, Invidia. I forgot for a moment... That was insensitive of me. Of course your sense of self isn't just defined by where you're from or who's related to you by blood—"

"No need to apologize. It's fine," insisted Invidia with a dismissive wave of her hand. "I'm not so easily offended. But I do think it's worth noting that a sense of belonging can be manifested, that roots can be planted and grow. I'm certainly not the only example of someone who has found family beyond blood relations. You're lucky with your family. You all get along, have similar values, and love and support each other. But..."

She shook her head.

"But what?" prompted Arínor.

"Well... sometimes love... even deep familial love... is not unconditional."

Invidia paused, letting her words sink into Arínor's prickling skin, like ice spiderwebbing through her veins and wrapping her blood in a cocoon of cold.

"I'm not saying that's the case with your family," said Invidia, her eyes imploring. "But times of fear test loyalties and blur lines. I just thought I'd point out there are other options if your family stops accepting you for who you are. There *are* people in Carmelle who would not only accept but celebrate your Celestial magic. Who wield Celestial magic together and are accepted for who they are. Who view Void magic as you do and are interested in its wider applications."

Cold shot up Arínor's spine like a stalagmite of ice, piercing her brain and raising the hairs on the back of her neck.

"Do you mean... Vashi?" Arínor whispered, and she angled her body away from Invidia.

Invidia shrugged, but her eyes locked on Arínor's. "I think you're right, that life is about sacrifice, but it's not so simple. You must make the right sacrifices, for the right reasons. I've heard that's why Vashi's use of Celestial magic requires sacrifice. He understands that sometimes the right sacrifices are those that benefit the greatest long-term good, even if it causes short-term heartache."

"I would never join with a man who chooses to engage in cruel sacrifices that unnecessarily hurt others, even if he accepts my Celestial magic and every other complex aspect of who I am," said Arínor, the cold numbing her body now frosting her voice.

"The morally correct answer, to be sure," replied Invidia with a sage nod of acquiescence. "Although... I sometimes wonder which is the more moral choice: sacrificing for one's own gain and happiness, or sacrificing for the happiness of a nation, a world. Say what you will about Vashi, but from what I can tell, he works to free Carmellians from the oppressive, restrictive paths the Keepers have set us on. Paths that displace rootless people like me, or non-Elemental magic folk like you. He understands fear of the unknown and uncontrollable is the greater enemy. His sacrifices are not selfish, made only for personal gain. How many of us can truly say that?"

Averting her gaze, Arínor attempted to swallow past her swollen tongue, her mouth bereft of saliva, barren as the Norance Dunes in the dry season. She bit her lip, tasting blood as screams echoed in her ears, as wide, terrified eyes found hers in the dark prison of her mind, pleading...

If she couldn't say her greatest sacrifices had been selfless... if her decisions had been fatal for others... what made her any better than Vashi?

Words failed Arínor. She merely nodded at Invidia, eyes downcast.

"Well. I should be getting on," said Invidia, standing up and brushing off her breeches. "See if Tessa's awake. No need for rash decisions now, but remember what I said. New paths present themselves all the time, but just because they're not well trodden doesn't mean venturing down them is the wrong choice. Even if Vashi is not the answer for you, I would still encourage you not to stifle your Celestial magic completely. Gifts like yours are rare. Suppressing your soul isn't just a risky sacrifice for you; it may hurt others as well. Deny the pressure of a soul's purpose too long, and it may implode."

Three

Arínor knew something was wrong the moment she flew over the mountain's shoulder and had to pivot around a plume of smoke. Blinking rapidly to clear the smoke burning her eyes, Arínor peered down at the valley, and her heart plummeted faster than one of her deep dives. She forgot to flap her wings, and her body dropped after her heart.

Her cottage was on fire.

Grey and white smoke billowed from the mountain-side wall, where she slept. And a few metres away, smaller curls of smoke rose out of the cracks around the ruby-and-sapphire oval door of—

No, no, please, no!

Throwing her wings out mid-drop, she transitioned into a smooth, arced glide to rebalance herself, then pumped her wings with rapid, powerful strokes and shot toward her cottage like an arrow.

She had taken her time with the flight home, detouring for a refreshing loop around the mountain peak. Had another one of her decisions proven fatal?

At the sight of her family huddled together a safe distance away from the wagon, Arínor's wings buckled, and she lost control. She spiralled to the ground, just managing to throw her wings out to slow herself down and get her clawed feet under her before she slammed into a grassy knoll and tumbled sideways, tucking her wings around her body. She couldn't breathe, all the air having been knocked out of her upon landing, and she shuddered as she forced her weak muscles to change, shape-shifting back into human form.

"*Arínor!*" her ma called out, choking on sobs as she sprinted over to her moaning daughter. "Oh, thank the stars, you're alive!"

"I was just going to say that to you," gasped Arínor, rolling up to her knees. "I saw the smoke, and I thought—I thought I had lost you."

Her ma pulled her into her lap like a child, stroking her hair like she was four, not thirty-four, but Arínor leaned into it, closing her eyes. In that moment, she wanted nothing more than the comfort of her mother's arms.

"What happened here?" asked Arínor, looking up not just at her ma but at the rest of her family, who had gathered around her, smiling through their tears.

"We don't know, exactly," said Aríetté, squeezing her husband's hand with one arm and pressing Anya close with the other. "Ruse woke us in the early hours of the morning, at dawn's first light, cawing and flapping in our faces until we got up. That's when we saw the fire in your room. Menkus and Ma ran in there to get you out, but they couldn't find you. We... we thought..."

Her younger sister trailed off, sniffling, and Arínor smiled at her through her own tears. "I'm sorry to scare everyone. Kerena came to get me in the middle of the night. She didn't want to wake anyone, but Tessa was having awful pains, and they needed my help."

"It doesn't matter. You're here now," said her ma, helping her to her unsteady feet. "Is Tessa all right?"

"Yes, she should be fine now," replied Arínor, brushing off her skirt. "Where's Ruse?"

"I have him!" squeaked Élí from behind Menkus, and he stepped into Arínor's view, Ruse clutching his arm with his talons. "We thought he would just fly away, but he refused to leave. I think he was waiting for you, Auntie Nor."

At the sight of Arínor, Ruse flapped to her shoulder and began chattering in her ear between affectionate nips.

"I'm sorry for scaring you too, Ruse," she whispered, stroking his feathers. Addressing her family again, she asked, "How did you manage to contain it all?"

Aríetté beamed at Anya, who clung to her mother's leg with wide ice-blue eyes, stark against a sooty face. "Turns out we have a wizard in the family."

Arínor gaped at her niece. "You did magic?"

Anya opened her mouth, but no words came out, so she closed it and nodded instead.

"She's still in shock," Aríetté explained gently. "But she saved us. Doused your room with a wave of water, quenching most of the fire. We tried putting it out ourselves first, with water from the well, once we had evacuated the children, but even though the fire wasn't really spreading past your room, we couldn't douse it. We were exhausted and coughing from the smoke inhalation, so we took a little too long getting out of your room at one point. I guess that worried Anya, because she marched right back inside the cottage, pushed us out of the room, held out her hands, and released an oceanic wave."

The worms wriggling in Arínor's stomach stilled, and she exhaled the breath she'd been holding. Elemental magic, then. Her niece would not have to suffer the vitriol thrown at Arínor.

"We are so lucky you were here. Thank you, Anya," said Arínor, giving her niece a shaky smile. "I don't think I left a candle burning or anything, so how did the fire start? Did you see anyone? How did the wagon catch fire?"

"We didn't see anyone," said Menkus, his voice slow and deliberate. "But..."

He looked toward the mountain side of the house, where smoke still drifted out of Arínor's bedroom window.

Arínor stepped toward her window, and her ma stepped with her, reaching out a hand as though to stop her daughter. When Arínor raised an eyebrow at her, she lowered her hand and said, "I guess you'll find out soon enough anyway."

Bile rose in her throat, and Arínor clutched her skirt with cold, shaking fingers as she looked down at the grass outside her window.

TRAITOR

The word had been carved into the earth as if a child had drawn it with a stick, but the lines were deep, the letters still glowing with embedded orange sparks.

"We tried to put it out," said her ma in a hushed whisper behind her, "but it won't be extinguished. It's like someone branded the word here with Fire magic."

Arínor swayed, clutching at the windowsill and blinking away the spots blurring her vision. It was all for her. The attack hadn't been an accident, or someone getting revenge on her whole family. It had been for *her*...

"Lís! Children!" cried a voice behind Menkus.

Gertie puffed up the hill, clutching her skirts with one hand and her chest with the other. "Thank the stars you're all safe. I was on my way anyway but then saw the smoke and ran... What *happened*?"

As her ma started to explain everything to Gertie, Arínor slipped away, sneaking inside the cottage to her room.

It was a wreck.

Shards of glass spilled across the room like scattered jewels. Most of the potions had been licked up by the flames—some may have even reacted with them to create explosions. Her shelves, desk, and store cupboard lay blackened and broken on the floor. Charred bits of feather and fabric littered the floor from the scorched bones of her mattress, and her bed frame had mostly been reduced to ash. As she stepped gingerly across the damp floor to the window, glass crunching beneath her boots, Arínor paused to pick up a twisted metal perch, still warm despite the wave that had drenched it. Ruse's perch.

Someone had targeted her room, setting fire to it with deliberate precision. The wagon's fire had seemed similarly precise and contained. Arietté had even said it seemed as though the fire had not been spreading to the rest of the cottage. Whoever had started the fire hadn't wanted to kill Arínor and her family—yet.

They had been sending a message.

Traitor.

Arínor had no doubt what that word meant. Not traitor to her family, or to the Armindí, but traitor to Carmelle for wielding Celestial magic. Maybe they thought her aligned with Vashi. Maybe they thought all who wielded Celestial magic inherently evil, and traitors to those who opposed the rising terror Vashi created. Either way, the warning was clear. She was no longer welcome here.

And if she didn't leave fast, her family might not be spared next time.

She reached to set Ruse's perch back on the blackened windowsill—and dropped it with a clatter instead. Her eyes latched on to something else perched on the sill.

The white-and-gold petal she had made with her Celestial magic.

Tears welled in her eyes. The back of her throat burned. Her chest heaved, panic rising in a tidal wave she couldn't stem.

Invidia.

Had she started the fire? An image of Invidia fiddling with a burn hole in her breeches flashed across Arínor's mind. She'd said she'd been tending her sick horse, but... could she have been starting the fire instead?

But Invidia respected her Celestial magic. She had been fascinated by Arínor's creation, had called it beautiful. And far from fearing Vashi, she had spoken of him with reverence and respect, like she was considering joining him. Or maybe she already had.

More than likely, Invidia had just picked up Arínor's dropped petal and decided to return it to her. It would have been difficult to arrive before Arínor even with her delay, but not impossible, especially if Invidia had used magic. When Invidia had seen the devastation, she may have decided to leave the petal for Arínor more discreetly. Or maybe leaving the petal hadn't even required her to set foot near the cottage. The extent of Elemental magic's capabilities and limitations often eluded Arínor, and she didn't know the specific strengths of Invidia's powers.

Perhaps the petal also served as a reminder for her to consider joining Vashi too.

Unless...

Invidia had asked her about the specific magic she had used to create the petal, and had deemed the use of Void magic fascinating, even indicating that Vashi shared her interest in using Void magic to create life and she would be welcome among his followers.

Could Vashi know about her Void magic?

She couldn't wait around to find out. If this wasn't just a malicious village prank but a more sinister warning linked to Vashi, her family was in far greater danger than she had realized.

After tucking the petal into the black pouch she still had in her pocket, she whirled to gather a few supplies and leave while her family was distracted with the repercussions of the fire—but she found Gertie standing in her bedroom doorway.

"Going somewhere?" Gertie asked calmly, hands in the pockets of her skirt.

Arínor hesitated but decided not to lie to Gertie. She would see right through it. "I'm leaving, and you can't stop me."

"You're right. I can't. I don't intend to fight you. I'd rather help than hinder."

"You want to help me leave?" repeated Arínor, not bothering to hide the shock coating her numb tongue. "But... how? I don't even know where I'm going. I just need to get away. Maybe Orinloth, or Éaloth, or even as far north as the ice fields of Froríz. I'd leave this world if I could, to keep my family safe."

"There are ways to leave this world, if you are determined to do so," offered Gertie.

Arínor stared at the older woman, stunned. "You mean... death?"

A piece of wet charcoal launched at her head.

"Of course not death, you daft moongazer!" admonished Gertie, balling up a piece of charred cloth this time.

"All right, sorry. Then what—oh! Do you mean portals?" Arínor asked. "But... I wouldn't even know where to look for one."

Gertie shrugged, commenting a little too casually, "Perhaps a flight around Harth would reveal answers."

"I've flown these mountains millions of times," said Arínor. "If there were something in the skies, I would have found it by now."

"That which you do not truly wish to see will remain hidden to you," said Gertie.

Narrowing her eyes at Gertie, Arínor assessed the situation. Her friend, elder, and business partner had no reason to lie to her about the location of a portal. Even if Gertie had an ulterior motive in helping Arínor leave that she wasn't sharing... did it matter? If she removed herself from this world entirely, she would not have to worry about the trouble the temptation of Celestial magic would land her in. She wouldn't run afoul of Vashi.

She wouldn't risk getting herself killed with one little slip of magic. She would be free, and her family would be safe. And if Gertie was wrong and there was no portal, she could still flee within Carmelle and at least save her family, if not herself.

"Will you explain my absence to my family? Let them know I'm alive, and I love them and hope to see them again some day?"

Gertie nodded and pulled Arínor in for a hug, patting her back. "I will. I wish you the best of luck, Arínor. Don't live in regret. And remember to be true to yourself."

"Take care, Gertie," Arínor managed through her wobbling chin and burning throat.

Arínor transformed into a lightning bird and flew out her bedroom window, and she didn't look back.

Arínor's screech reverberated off Harth's jagged cliffs, a high-pitched scream of rage that continued to echo her frustration back at her. She had circled these cliffs a dozen times already, eyes peeled for any anomaly among the clouds, any gaping hole or door or shimmer that could possibly be a portal. She had even considered flying straight at the rock face and hoping she would vanish through, like diving into water, challenging Gertie's theory that if she wanted to find it badly enough, it would reveal itself to her. But she didn't quite feel like testing the immortality of the Armindí yet.

I'll just fly around one more time, she thought, angling her wings to soar through the crevice between a smooth cliff face and a thick, crooked spire jutting up from an outcrop of rock. *One more time, and then—*

Her wingtip brushed against something as she exited the crevice. Something close to the spire but further out into open air. Arínor turned and hovered by the spire, facing the high clouds layering the sky above her and the striated wisps floating toward the peak behind her. She squinted at the air where her wing had brushed something solid, tilting her head.

There.

An infinitesimal ripple, a shimmer not quite the same as the air around it...

She poked it with her wingtip.

An obsidian step materialized, hovering in mid-air, bereft of support.

Heart racing, Arínor tried to land on it, slipped when her claws couldn't get a grip on the smooth stone, and pitched forward. Her beak smacked into another invisible solid entity, and she nearly fell off the step from the dizzying pain. Splaying her toes wide and lowering her torso, she regained her balance in time to see the second slick step materialize where she had injured her beak.

Taking a deep breath, she closed her eyes and shape-shifted into her more sure-footed human form.

An action she regretted as soon as she opened her eyes to the sight of nothing but empty sky below her feet. Empty sky, and at the furthest reaches of her vision, the jagged sawtooth peaks of the mountain's shoulder. No wings to catch her fall. No cushion or shield against inevitable death. Just a free fall into nothingness.

Dizzy swirls swam in her head; blood pounded in her chest and drummed a beat to the ringing in her ears; and nausea rose from her stomach to her throat. She wobbled and only saved herself from falling off by lurching to the next step and bending her knees, widening her stance and throwing her arms out for balance.

Arínor repeated the steps of this wobbly ascension, reaching out tentatively with her toes until she touched the next step and it materialized, then lurching forward and regaining her balance. She kept her eyes fixed on her feet and the steps, not daring to look beyond at the fathomless drop below. Though the day was overcast but not stormy, wind still whipped her clothes and howled in her ears at this elevation.

Finally, after at least a dozen steps, Arínor placed her foot on the last one—and an ebony door frame materialized, connected to the last obsidian step. Black smoke billowed in the doorframe, swirling and rippling within its confines like a waving veil.

A portal.

Arínor had only ever heard of these in stories, tales passed down around a fire, of doorways to other worlds. Places with different people, creatures, societies, languages, laws... was she really ready for such a drastic change? Was she ready to uproot everything she knew, everything she had clung to for the last thirty years?

No. She would never be ready for that.

But maybe you were never ready for the sacrifices that defined you.

Sacrifices like Invidia had alluded to, ones worth making even if the consequences were dire, because they benefited so many more lives than her own. She could save her family. She could help Carmelle by not aiding Vashi with her Void magic.

Maybe she could even atone for her partner's death.

Or I could lose myself and regret it forever, like Gertie said.

But Gertie had told her about the portal. And though she knew her family would miss her, as she would miss them, at least Gertie could explain. She had to trust they would understand her choice. A sacrifice necessary for their safety, but if Arínor was honest with herself, for her own happiness as well. She didn't want to live in fear of ever using her Celestial magic, and she didn't want to give it up entirely. Carmelle was no longer safe for people with Celestial magic, and she didn't want to join Vashi for protection. Maybe Invidia was right. Maybe his intentions were misunderstood, lumped in with society's blind fear of the unknown. But she didn't have enough information to know if that was true, and she couldn't risk others to find out.

But she could take risks herself.

Arínor reached her hand toward the black smoke and halted with it poised an inch away from the twirling tendrils. She didn't know what awaited her on the other side of this portal. Whether she would still be able to use her magic or would just have to walk back through to Carmelle, as she had heard of others doing. She didn't know if she could ever belong.

But she did not fear the unknown.

She embraced it.

Arínor plunged her hand into the black mist.

Four

November 1769, Boston, Massachusetts

The pause in their argument allowed Clemency the chance to twiddle her pencil between her fingers, working the cramps out of her hand before scribbling fiercely again when a retort had been fired.

"I'm not paying a tax on paper. It's criminal, and I won't be bullied into it," protested the captain of the merchant vessel docked at Long Wharf, in front of the bench where Clemency sat taking notes on his heated debate with a British soldier. His ship scraped against the dock with every roll of the wind-rippled waves, rocking the crew members unloading crates.

"No, what's criminal is you refusing to pay, and you will be penalized for it," repeated the soldier, gritting his teeth to bite back the last of his rapidly waning patience.

"These damned taxes will be the King's downfall, mark my words!" cried the captain, the empty threat his only weapon against the musket in the soldier's hands. Hatred burned in his eyes, fuel to stir the pot of mutiny and rebellion.

Clemency wove words of the oppressed rising up to seize their freedom, wielding them like a sword, imagining the end of tyranny through the assassination of King George, like in Shakespeare's *Julius Caeser*.

"Drat!" Clemency cursed at the snap of her pencil tip breaking.

Both the captain and soldier turned to her with raised eyebrows and wide eyes that quickly narrowed from shock to suspicion.

"What are you writing there?" the soldier asked.

"A letter to a friend," replied Clemency with smooth nonchalance.

"On paper we have to pay extra for with our hard-earned money because of King George's ridiculous, power-hungry taxes," growled the captain.

"I quite agree," said Clemency. "The Townshend Acts are an outrageous joke and will soon meet the same fate as the Stamp Act before them. Our loathing for taxation has only increased."

"What would *you* know about it?" the captain sneered. "You're just a woman. The letter to your friend is probably a compendium of small-minded gossip."

His derisive gesture to Clemency's meticulous notes detailing the nuances of their precarious political position scalded her blood. She had taken his side, shown her political knowledge, and had still been treated like a foul sludge he had sullied new shoes in. A stronger woman might not let comments like that bother her, secure behind the wall men bricked between them and not caring if it was built higher or crumbled. But Clemency had never been able to brush others' opinions and comments off her shoulder as though they were inconsequential crumbs. Their comments clung to her like burrs, prickling and unshakable.

Hope's tenuous fluctuation taunted Clemency, inflating with the promise of freedom and deflating whenever she remembered freedom for the Patriots would not mean freedom for women. But change had to start somewhere, so she would bide her time fighting for one cause at a time.

"It's certainly a compendium of the small-minded," retorted Clemency, sliding her pencil and paper through the slit in her skirt to tuck them into the pocket tied beneath. She stood and turned her back on the captain's reddening face, stopping short to avoid colliding with a man's chest.

"Finished!" her husband, Sampson, declared, and she flicked her eyes from his chest to his face to see his smile kindling his amber eyes. "Just in time for supper. I'm starved. Did inspiration strike today?"

"Long Wharf continues to prove a steady fountain of inspiration from which I drink, even if the taste is sometimes bitter," replied Clemency, taking Sampson's offered arm and strolling away from the captain and soldier. Their argument resumed behind her, devolving into shouts that carried above the gentle chatter of people strolling down the wharf or milling about the shops lining one side.

"How ominous," teased Sampson with a wink. "Do I need to defend your honour?"

"My honour has not been compromised, just my pride."

Sampson slowed, turning to study her eyes with a slight frown. "What happened?"

"It's nothing, really. Just a reminder that my voice is only as strong as my husband's. Lucky for me, my husband's voice is stronger than most." She smiled up at him, trying to coax her lips to stretch beyond the thin, straight line flattening them.

Gently pinching her chin between his forefinger and thumb, Sampson tilted it upward and lowered his head, closing the head-height gap while still toeing the line of propriety. Clemency flicked her gaze to the peripheries of her vision to ensure no one observed their intimate position too closely.

"You don't need my voice to be heard, Clemency," Sampson assured her, his voice tender and earnest. "Your voice was stronger than mine before we wed and has only grown more powerful. People will listen to it if you give them the chance."

"But how to get them to listen when I am dismissed as soon as I open my mouth because I am a woman?" Clemency mused aloud. "The chance has been given, but only you have taken it."

"And I am a man forever changed because of it," said Sampson. "I believe in you and value your views, but it's not my opinion that matters, nor anyone else's. It's yours."

If only that were true, Clemency thought, but she kept that truth to herself, knowing further debate would be superfluous.

Clemency offered her husband a small smile, pouring all her adoration for him into that simple gesture. It wasn't his fault his words carried no more weight than a lover's sweet nothings. She knew he believed them to be true and loved him for his innocent optimism.

"So, you finished your task as well?" Clemency asked Sampson as they left the wharf for King Street.

"For now," he replied, and from the pity in his eyes, Clemency knew her disappointment had leaked through the cracks in her mask of indifference. She attempted to patch the leaks as panic clamped her chest and clawed up her throat.

Fixing her gaze on the minute hand of the clock mounted above the balcony on the front of the brick Town House, Clemency asked, "How long?"

"They want me to stay for another month or two," said Sampson, his tone gentle and careful, as though cradling a cannonball about to be loaded into a cannon. "I know it's hard on you. I'm sorry. I'll return as soon as I can—"

"It's fine," Clemency interjected before he could utter any more sympathetic words. Each one grated on her nerves and jolted her heart, stinging more because she knew he truly did empathize with her feelings but was still bound by his duty to the Massachusetts House of Representatives and therefore could do nothing to lessen his time away from their home in Plymouth. "The children and I will be fine."

She tried to take a deep breath, to force her lungs to expand to their full capacity despite the pressure weighing on her chest like a dragon curled over her heart, but she still had to halt, swaying where she stood in the middle of the street while people brushed past and horse-drawn wagons trundled by. Another month or two of sleepless nights, of staring out her window at the silver-tipped ebony river flowing behind their house, trying to soothe nightmares of fire with water, only to be drawn to the water's depths, sinking into a new fear of heads slipping beneath the innocent glint of its moonlit surface, never to emerge.

Sampson took her hands in his, perhaps seeing the midnight depths of the river reflected in the pupils of her wide, glazed eyes. "You're always less anxious when you have a purpose. Something to distract and engage that active mind of yours. Perhaps there is a cause you could support, or something in your notes you could expand upon."

Clemency's unseeing eyes refocused on the blood-red coats of a trio of British soldiers heading into the Bunch-of-Grapes tavern near the wharf's head, and an idea bubbled at the back of her mind, percolating like a simmering antidote.

"Yes... yes, you're right. There is much I can accomplish still while you are away. I'll start by hosting a gathering, see if I can't gauge the status of our friends' political views. I wonder if I might get a note to Mr. and Mrs. Adams while I'm here..."

She looked around the street for a store that might sell stationery.

Sampson chuckled, kissing her hand affectionately. "It never takes you long to find renewed purpose, my dear. I so admire that in you. As it so happens, I'll be seeing Mr. Adams tomorrow. We need to consult a lawyer, so I can hand-deliver the note. Unless you want to take it to Brattle Street yourself."

"You know, I would like to see Mrs. Adams again. I'll try to get it to her before I leave tomorrow," said Clemency, her stronger voice reflecting the strength returning to her limbs and lungs. The fog misting her thoughts cleared, and she added, "Why don't you secure a carriage for us and arrange for my transportation while I procure what I need to send invitations? I remember a little shop on the next street down that should have what I need."

"I'll meet you back here in half an hour," Sampson agreed.

A little bell clanged as Clemency opened the door of the small shop, and the man at the counter greeted her with a respectful bob of his head. She inclined her head in return, then directed her attention to the shelves lining the shop from floor to ceiling. Though the shop was not crowded, she still had to sidle past a woman with a black skirt, examining a set of glass vials in the narrow aisle between display tables, to reach the paper stacked neatly in rows along one wall. After selecting paper appropriate for invitations and wax, Clemency shuffled to the counter and laid her purchases before the proprietor.

"Find everything you were looking for, ma'am?" the shop owner asked.

"Yes, thank you," replied Clemency. "Oh, wait! Hold on. I need a quill and ink."

She turned to grab a white quill and a bottle of black ink while he started tallying her purchases, then reached into her pocket for coins once she had placed them on the counter. She handed him a few coins, but he shook his head.

"Not quite enough, ma'am. You didn't account for the tax."

Clemency chewed the inside of her cheek and counted to three before replying, "Ah, yes. A tax on paper. We wouldn't want to upset the British by not paying that."

She should have counted to ten. Sarcasm dripped like molasses from every word.

Pink splotches stained the man's cheeks. "It's not your place to have an opinion, *ma'am*."

"Excuse me, *sir*, but she has just as much right to an opinion as you," said the woman in the black skirt, approaching the counter. Her raven hair was bundled atop her head like a bird's nest, wisps fanning out like feathers instead of curled and coiffed, and her grey eyes darkened like a thundercloud.

"The only opinion women have a right to is the one the men in their lives tell them to have. You'd both do best to remember that, *now*." The proprietor's pink cheeks deepened to puce, his jowls quivering.

"I'd rather eat horseshit than regurgitate a man's opinion over my own," the woman said coldly. Clemency's eyes widened at her vehemency, and yet admiration warmed her chest at her bold defence of women.

The warmth evaporated in the next moment as the man shouted, "OUT! Get out of my shop, and don't come back."

"Gladly," said the woman, and she turned on her heel to leave.

"Oh, b-but I really do need—" stammered Clemency, flustered as she reached back toward the counter and her writing supplies.

"Forget it," said the woman over her shoulder, cutting Clemency off. "I know of another shop with better prices *and* respect for women's opinions."

"Really?" Clemency asked, stunned. The woman didn't answer as she slammed the door open and stormed out.

Clemency hurried after her, glancing one last time over her shoulder at the abandoned stationery under the watchful eye of the irate owner.

Arínor charged into the street, chest heaving and heart pounding in her ears. It had taken all her control not to put a retribution curse on the man and let him suffer the consequences of his prejudices for the rest of his life. She almost regretted the language curse she had put on herself, because if she hadn't enabled her ears to understand and translate foreign languages, she wouldn't have understood his derogatory comments. But she also would not have been able to *speak* foreign languages and defend that woman—an action she could not regret, even if she now had to find somewhere else to purchase the vials Meredith had asked her to find.

"Where's the shop you spoke of?" the woman asked as Arínor paused at the end of the street, surveying the strange, rectangular, many-windowed buildings and men hurrying in and out of them, dressed in odd fashions she still hadn't become accustomed to after two weeks in this bustling town. She angled her face so the woman couldn't see her darting eyes as she tried to recall the route to the apothecary.

Grimacing, Arínor squared her shoulders and faced the woman. "I don't know. A shop like that may exist, but if it does, I don't know about it. I'm sorry. I shouldn't have said that and gotten your hopes up. I was just so angry and wanted him to think we had the upper hand."

"Oh." The woman's shoulders slumped, and she cast her cobalt-blue eyes down to her shoes. The slick sandy ringlets twisting down from her neat coiffure bobbed with the movement, and her fingers clutched the copper fabric of her wide skirt. "I understand. I was angry too. I just... usually bite my tongue."

"But why?" Arínor asked. "Treating a woman like that is disgusting."

"I agree, but there's nothing to gain by complaining about it. Men always treat women as inferior. That's just how it is. I prefer the ones who are more respectful, of course, but it wouldn't be very feminine of me to rage at every man I meet. Not that you were raging—I didn't mean to imply that. It was nice of you to try and defend me. I do appreciate it."

"And being feminine is more important to you than not being treated like vermin?" Arínor asked. "Women just... accept this treatment here?"

"Here?"

Too late Arínor bit her tongue.

"Where are you from?" the woman asked, her eyes narrowing.

"Far from here," Arínor answered evasively. "Where women are treated as equals and with respect. I'm certainly better understanding the plights of some of the women who have come into the apothecary where I just started working."

"Sounds like a fairy tale," said the woman. Then she added with a wry twist of her lips, "Though far from being treated equally, the women in Perrault's fairy tales needed magical aids to have a happy life. I guess most of us are still just waiting for our fairy godmother."

Arínor almost choked on her own saliva at the mention of magic and fairies. She had no idea what fairy tales the woman referred to, but she wondered if this Perrault had seen a fairy who had wandered through a portal or witnessed magic without knowing it. She cleared her throat and said, "Sorry to disappoint—again—but I'm not a fairy godmother. But if you ever want suggestions on how to stop biting your tongue and use your voice, I'd be happy to oblige."

An idea gleamed in the woman's blue eyes, sparkling like sunlight dancing on water, and Arínor's stomach fluttered.

"I'm hosting a gathering of like-minded folk, a meeting of revolutionary ideas and ideals. Would you be interested in coming—I'm sorry I didn't catch your name. What was it?"

"Arínor. Yours?"

The woman opened her mouth to reply, shook her head as though changing her mind, then said, "Clemency."

"Nice to meet you, Clemency," said Arínor with a grin. "I don't have many friends yet, so it would be nice to meet more people who share similar ideals. Where is this gathering?"

"At my house in Plymouth..." Clemency's smile slipped, and the sparkle in her eyes dulled. A crease wrinkled the gap between her eyebrows. "Now that I say it aloud, my idea doesn't seem so brilliant. Plymouth is too far from Boston to be convenient. Maybe we can meet up when I'm in Boston next. I return to Plymouth tomorrow."

The fluttering wings brushing Arínor's stomach stilled. She didn't know where Plymouth was, or if she could get there in a timely fashion, but a knot tightened in her chest at the thought of not seeing Clemency again—of giving up the first real connection she had found in this world.

"I can't promise that I can get there, but I can try," said Arínor. "How would I find it?"

"Oh, of course, I haven't written the invitations yet. That's what I needed the paper for... Hold on. I have something."

She reached into a pocket at her waist and extracted a folded piece of paper and a small writing tool. Tearing off a corner of the paper, she scribbled something on it and handed it to Arínor.

"My address, and the date and time of the gathering," said Clemency. "Just in case. I hope to see you again, Arínor."

Before Arínor could wrap her tongue around her half-formed acquiescence, Clemency had glanced at the big, numbered contraption on a building, squeaked "I must go!" and hurried off down the street, lifting her skirts a little to free her feet.

Arínor watched her dodge excrement on the road for a moment before turning in the direction she hoped led to the apothecary. Her mind reeled, dizzy from the invigorating rush of purpose flooding her veins. For the first time since leaving Carmelle, she had felt a connection with someone, a sisterhood. It was an intoxicating feeling, like a plant leaning into the sun's warm rays, a welcome warmth after weeks of nothing but shadows and doubt.

When she had walked through the portal into open air and had immediately started plunging toward the churning, frothy grey waters of the ocean below, her heart had plummeted faster than her body. As she had transformed into a lightning bird in mid-air and skimmed the waves with her wings, she couldn't help but dread the loneliness that awaited her. She had never been truly alone for any length of time, without friends, family, or lovers. The nomadic lifestyle of the Armindí coupled with the primal instincts of a lightning bird had taught her enough survival skills that she felt she could at least survive—but could she ever thrive without the comfort and solace of a companion? Could the walls of her mind hold and keep unwanted memories locked away?

After a week of scavenging food along the coast and roosting in trees or in crevices of rocky cliffs as a lightning bird and finding nothing but small villages and scowling faces, she had decided to fly south a little, hoping to find a city she could get lost in, somewhere with a bigger population and more opportunities for earning meals in her human form. That was when she had found Boston, a sprawling town with low buildings and pointy spires, none of which belonged to palaces like the one in Carenthia. But the ships gathering in the harbour like a conspiracy of ravens looked akin to the ships she'd seen crowding the Carenth-hild, carrying with them the promise of trade, business, and opportunity, so she had decided to chance it.

Earth had proven both fascinating and underwhelming at the same time thus far, full of the wondrous and mundane, the scales tipping one way or another, never balanced.

She had been lucky to stumble across the apothecary only a few days after settling in Boston, and even more lucky that the proprietor's wife, Meredith, had allowed her the opportunity to show her skills and prove useful. But though using the skill set she had spent years honing was rewarding, the swell of her chest and flutter in her stomach told her this chance meeting with Clemency may have been more fortuitous. A non-linear path to a greater purpose. A way to help women not just with herbal remedies and medicinal needs but with something Arínor had always taken for granted in Carmelle: equality.

As Arínor turned down another side street, recognizing the pub on the corner now, she reflected that perhaps the sacrifice of leaving her family and home world behind served a greater purpose, as Invidia had suggested. Perhaps her loss meant helping to breathe renewed vigor into so many women who needed to hear their worth was not measured and restricted by their gender.

She could start by helping Clemency.

She would find a wagon or horse to transport her to Plymouth.

And if those failed, she had wings.

Five

"We must be going, Clemency, dear, but it was a lovely evening," her closest friend Abigail Adams assured her, clasping her hand in thanks.

"Yes, illuminating conversation, as always," agreed her husband John, shrugging on his cloak. "Tensions certainly are rising on all fronts. What you witnessed on Long Wharf is increasingly commonplace, but it's only a matter of time before we have another Liberty Affair on our hands. You know I'm not entirely opposed to Loyalist sentiments, but it does seem like two separate brewing thunderclouds set on a collision course—the resulting storm is bound to be catastrophic. There's much to think about, indeed."

Clemency glanced out the window at the torrential downpour and hunched her shoulders against the involuntary shiver that rippled across her neck. "I expect the voyage to independence to be tumultuous, but I'm ready to weather the storm."

"As am I!" Mr. Samuel Adams called from a few feet away, evidently eavesdropping on their goodbye.

Though Clemency chuckled amiably, she glanced at the darkness beyond the glistening rivulets streaming down the window again and chewed her lip. She hadn't really expected Arínor to appear—it had been a ridiculous ask, an impulsive idea bordering on impetuous—but her chest still constricted, her heart shrivelling a little, in her absence. A voice confident in a woman's right to express her opinions might have emboldened Clemency's own voice and prompted her to express the more radical views she withheld to retain her femininity. But their conversation last week still lingered in her mind and had inspired her to push propriety boundaries more tonight.

After John and Abigail left, followed by a local couple from Plymouth, the gathering started to look a little thin. Clemency fanned herself with an imported lace fan, heat creeping up her cheeks even more at the irony, even if it had been imported before the new tax laws. She glanced at the deepening sky again, fingers tingling and breath quickening. Echoing chatter quieted to hushed murmurs, and a few more guests took their leave.

Offers of more drinks were declined, and the last guests expressed their regrets that they must leave. They started gathering their cloaks, and Clemency pressed a hand to her tightening chest. Soon she would be alone in a house of sleeping occupants, with only silence for company.

A series of knocks pounded at the door, heavy and sporadic as though the knocker second-guessed their decision halfway through. The few remaining guests looked around at each other, small creases puckering their brows, probably asking themselves the same question reverberating in Clemency's head: *Who joins a gathering at this hour as all the guests are leaving?*

A moment later, her butler Thompson escorted a sopping-wet Arínor into the room, water dripping from her ebony cloak and bedraggled hair. A puddle formed beneath her muddy boots.

Relief seeped into Clemency's skin like a cold compress, and she snapped her fan shut.

"I'm sorry," Arínor said before the lingering gasps had time to marinate in the silence. "The wagon's wheel got stuck in the mud. It took ages to free, and then the driver got lost in the rainy dark, and—"

"No need to apologize. These things happen. You've missed the gathering, I'm afraid. The last guests were just leaving," said Clemency, gesturing at the men and women donning their cloaks, "but do stay for some chocolate at least."

"Oh, I don't know. I don't want to be a bother," Arínor began, but Clemency waved away her protests.

"Thompson, please fetch some chocolate and bring it to the drawing room so our guest can warm up by the fire," Clemency instructed her butler.

Thompson hurried to the kitchen, and Clemency turned to the last guests of her gathering while Arínor continued to stand there dripping awkwardly. "Thank you so much for coming, everyone. I hope to see you back here soon."

When the last guest had closed the door behind them, Clemency turned to Arínor and grinned. "Are you sure you didn't swim here?"

"I may as well have. It would have saved time," Arínor muttered, removing her cloak with careful precision to avoid splashing any of the furniture or candles. "You don't have to entertain me, you know. I know it's late, and you were probably hoping to sleep. I wasn't even going to knock, but I wanted to apologize and let you know I was in town so we could arrange to meet another time, maybe."

"Don't be silly. It's not that late, and you need to dry off. And I'd be glad of the company," Clemency added over her shoulder as she led the way into the drawing room. A cozy fire crackled in the stone fireplace, beckoning them closer. Arínor perched on the edge of the sofa, reaching her wrinkled fingers toward the flames, and Clemency sank into Sampson's armchair, unable to stop a contented sigh escaping her lips. "The truth is I rather loathe being alone when my husband is away. I mean, I'm not *alone*, of course. I have the servants, and my five children—they're asleep right now—but I *feel* alone."

A peculiar expression froze Arínor's face, cheekbones slackened and lips parted slightly as though stunned with a tinge of disappointment, but Clemency couldn't quite place why she averted her eyes to the fire. Did

Clemency's vulnerability with a stranger make Arínor uncomfortable? Maybe Clemency had mistaken her confidence for a confidant.

"Sorry, I shouldn't speak of such—"

"Don't be sorry. I'm glad you told me how you feel," Arínor interrupted hurriedly, meeting her eyes again. "I've always been an advocate for speaking your mind, and emotions are no exception to that. I also understand completely. I, too, loathe being alone. Trapped with your own thoughts, no presence to comfort you, even if it's just with their silent proximity. You imagine the worst, worry you won't be able to handle the worst on your own, that your character will be tested, and you'll be found wanting."

"*Yes,*" breathed Clemency, staring at Arínor's blurry face through watery eyes. Hearing her fears spoken aloud so precisely left her breathless with exhilaration and terror.

"I've been away from my family for a few weeks now," said Arínor, her hands fluttering in her lap as though she was unsure what to do with them. "It has been... difficult. I appreciate you asking me here tonight. I'm sorry I missed the meeting."

"Don't be," said Clemency, looking up as Thompson shuffled over to them bearing a tray. He set it down on the polished oak table between them, and both Clemency and Arínor thanked him at the same time.

After bobbing his head in acknowledgement, Thompson padded off to the kitchen again. "It wasn't revolutionary, at least not in terms of new actionable discussions. But it still feels better to talk about what's going on than ignore it and pretend the political climate is not fraught with towers of powder kegs one torch away from exploding. Chocolate?"

"I must confess, I've never had chocolate before, but I'd be happy to try it," said Arínor.

"It's divine," Clemency assured her. "We're trying to boycott as many British imports as possible to show our opposition to the taxation, so we are finding substitutes for tea. I like coffee too, but not before bed. Chocolate is more soothing. I think I like it even better than tea. Especially if you add a little whisky—another substitute we're trying instead of rum. This one is locally made. Can I tempt you?"

Arínor nodded, and Clemency poured her a cup of chocolate with a splash of whisky, leaning across the space between them to hand it to her. She brushed Arínor's fingers slightly as the cup exchanged hands, and she thought Arínor stiffened a little.

"Did you travel here alone, then? Is your husband working?" Clemency asked, deciding to be blunt instead of dancing around Arínor's statement of not seeing her family for a few weeks.

"I travelled here alone, yes. I'm not married," replied Arínor, rubbing her thumb along the handle of her teacup. "I guess I'm not very conforming. I work at an apothecary in Boston, but after I met you, I started chatting with the proprietor's wife, Meredith, and it turns out she has a cousin in Plymouth who helps women in need, and she was looking for someone to assist with a few upcoming births. I told her I had some experience, and her cousin said she would love my help. I'll be staying with her for a while."

Clemency sat up straighter, eyes wide. "You'll be staying in Plymouth?"

"Is... that all right?" Arínor asked, swallowing her chocolate with apparent difficulty.

"That's wonderful! Having a friend nearby will be so lovely... well, if you think so," added Clemency awkwardly, realizing she was being presumptuous calling Arínor a friend.

"It will be lovely indeed," Arínor said with a smile that made her smoky-grey eyes shine silver.

Clemency's cheeks warmed, though that could have just been the whisky.

"You seem intelligent, open to change, and passionate about creating a better world. I see the fire in your eyes when you talk about women's inequality or freeing your people from British tyranny. I admire that kind of purpose and passion for a cause. I've never fought for anything like that."

Cocking her head at Arínor, Clemency crooked her lips at one corner. "I doubt that."

"It's true," Arínor insisted.

"Well then, maybe we should fight together," said Clemency, taking another emboldening sip of her whisky-chocolate.

"We could set something up for women," said Arínor, her voice rising in excitement. "I can help you, if you want to try. You could reach out to your friends and contacts who might be interested, and I could talk to Meredith's cousin and see if any women she helps would like to come. Change must start somewhere, right? We could be that starting point."

Clemency lowered her cup to the saucer and slowly set it down on the tray, staring into the fire. She wasn't delusional. She knew she couldn't revolutionize women's rights. She wasn't even sure if she wanted to. She had her husband and children to think about, and a reputable social standing in an influential circle of friends she had carefully cultivated, positioning herself to share intelligent ideas and engage in important political movements while still maintaining her femininity. But Arínor was right that change had to start somewhere. It may be a long, arduous road. It may never come to fruition. But sometimes if you started the call, others took it up. And like the cry to overthrow British rule, it could rise to a roar, a clamouring that could not be ignored.

Clemency locked eyes with Arínor and said, "I'm in."

"Arínor, are you done with that mixture?" Molly bellowed from upstairs.

"Almost! I just have one more ingredient to add!" Arínor called, but Molly's feet thundered down the stairs before she had finished her sentence, and soon she could feel the pierce of her sharp eyes on the back of her neck as she peered over her shoulder at the mixture Arínor stirred.

"More mugwort," she instructed.

Arínor added a pinch more atop the mistletoe she had just added, careful not to overdo it.

"Hannah's expecting us soon, so we must hurry," said Molly, packing a basket full of herbs, salves, clean cloths, and other items of comfort and pain relief.

"This will be ready in two minutes," said Arínor, stirring more vigorously.

"Here, have a quick bite while you're stirring," insisted Molly, and she gestured for Arínor to open her mouth so she could shove a piece of bread into it.

Arínor obliged without complaint, knowing she wouldn't get the chance to eat again until late that night.

Arínor had settled into a routine with Meredith's cousin Molly, a comfortable and familiar one resembling the bustling fluidity of her home and family business back on Arwé. They assisted the local doctor with complications in women's health, and in her free time, Arínor visited Clemency, planning their next women's meeting.

The first one they had tried to hold, only a week after agreeing to plan a meeting, had predictably failed. The few women they had managed to contact had not shown up, and one of Clemency's five sons had been unable to sleep, sneaking away from his nanny to seek the comfort of his mother's arms. Clemency had read him a story by the fire, stroking his hair until his eyelids had drooped, then carried him up to bed. She had returned with fresh determination burning in her eyes, declaring that she would not be deterred. Consoling themselves with more chocolate and whisky, they had spent the evening dreaming up ways to recruit women without scaring them, easing them into such a radical idea. They had agreed to hold the next meeting a month from then, in January. A fresh start to a fresh year, giving them almost a month to prepare.

Now, three weeks later, hope inflated Arínor's chest at their prospects. She had planted the seed in conversations with a few of the women she had met, keeping her tone light but her message clear, and they had seemed interested. Clemency had reported that a few of her acquaintances had shared their sentiments in letters, though she wasn't sure if any of them would be able to attend a meeting in person without their husbands' permission—which they were unlikely to receive. But interest was a start, and shared sentiments in letters still held weight.

And the reflected light of the flames dancing in Clemency's eyes during their fireside chats, igniting her smouldering determination, was entrancing. Intoxicating. She—

"Arínor, snap out of it! That's done!" Molly admonished.

Arínor jumped and dropped the spoon. It clattered to the wooden table and fell to the floor, where Molly's cat, Tundra, licked it clean.

"Sorry!"

Arínor poured the mixture into a bottle, added it to Molly's basket, and hurried out the door in Molly's wake.

When they arrived at Hannah's, Molly pounded on the door, but no one answered.

"Miss Davis?" Molly called. She pressed her ear to the door. "Hannah? I'm coming in."

After pushing open the unlocked door, Molly hurried inside, and Arínor followed.

In a bedroom off the kitchen, they found Hannah, curled on her side with her knees drawn to her chest, tears rolling down her cheeks as she rocked herself on the bed.

"It's all right now, Hannah. Here we are," said Molly, rubbing her back and fumbling with the basket. "Pass me the mixture, Arínor."

Arínor uncorked the bottle she had just filled and poured a small measure onto a spoon. She passed it to Molly, who helped Hannah swallow it, rubbing soothing circles on her back the whole time. "This will help the pain, dear, and hopefully help regulate your cycle a bit better. Your cramps are some of the worst I've seen, but we hope this will help ease the worst of them."

Though Hannah couldn't speak, Arínor caught a small nod beneath the bend of her arms, now cradling her head. The thrum of Arínor's core pulsed, beckoning to be embraced. She could sense a deep darkness in Hannah, a blotch of emptiness like a seeping ink stain. A thread of her Void magic waved tantalizingly, and she thought of the glass petal she had breathed life into. What if she could dissolve the stain, stitch the void's decaying darkness together instead of letting it spread?

Arínor had tested her magic in small, subtle ways since coming to Earth—redirecting moonlight to illuminate Clemency's desk so she could see the letters she wrote to her friends Martha and Catharine better or sneaking a mote of stardust into a tincture she made for Molly in the middle of the night, to increase its potency—but she hadn't tried to replicate the petal yet. She had thought about it, though, unable to get the idea of healing with Void magic out of her mind. She was sure she could do it. The theory aligned with everything she had tested on inanimate objects in Carmelle, every attempt at creating life or filling voids rendered successful.

Hannah had already swallowed the mixture, and if Molly didn't exactly believe it would cure her, she did believe it would help. Arínor didn't think her Void magic would be a cure either. But it might heal more effectively than herbal remedies, and if Molly assumed her mixture had been more potent than anticipated... was there any harm in that?

Taking a deep breath to steady her shaking fingers, Arínor closed her eyes and channelled a thin thread of Void magic toward the black stain marring Hannah's insides, first emptying it of the decay, then knitting it together and smoothing it out until the gnawing, jagged emptiness had been filled.

Hannah's eyes widened, and she gasped. Uncurling her spine, she slowly sat up, resting a hand lightly on her lower abdomen and flicking her gaze between Molly and Arínor.

"The pain... it's gone. It feels... I feel... that mixture... I don't know what you gave me, but it worked. It worked!" Hannah's awed voice cracked as her eyes crinkled against the well of tears. "Thank you."

Tears pricked Arínor's eyes too. She had done it. She had used Void magic to heal. Her Celestial magic wasn't a curse. It was a gift.

Carmellians hadn't been able to see that. They hadn't given her the chance to show them. They had let their fear of the unknown blind them to the possibilities of what could be, reducing her to single-word labels. Corrupt. Evil. Traitor.

Here, her controversial Celestial magic could earn her a new label.

Healer.

Six

December 25, 1769

My dearest Sam,

I miss you.

A three-word combination more potent than "I love you."

I can see you rolling your eyes and shaking your head at such a ridiculous, bold statement. Who am I to defy the most power-ful phrase in the English language, to disagree with the finest poets and playwrights in history? To spit in the face of Shake-speare's sonnets, to admit that impediments do in fact hinder the marriage of true minds. Distance, absence, time—all are proven impediments to even the most ardent love. But to miss someone is proof that absence has not faded your love like a waning moon, but that love has become your guiding star, your ever-fixèd mark. Love leaves you in equal parts pain and joy, emptying and filling you like a well. When the person you love is with you, you are whole, complete. When they are gone, you are hollow, a broken piece waiting to be glued back together.

You try to fill the void with distractions, but it is a yawning, bottomless pit, with three words reverberating between its walls: I miss you.

And yet "I miss you" has probably lost all meaning to you, worn ragged from over-use, just as "I love you" starts to lose its meaning when uttered too often. But it is the only way I know how to express this simultaneous emptiness and longing as I sit here with my mulled wine and think of you. I think of you sitting beside me, laughing at the memory of Winslow's face as he tried to remember his lines in the play the children put on for us this Christmas. I think of you trying to steal a kiss under the mistletoe.

Since you are not here, the only thing I can do is try to fill the void with distractions. I know I already mentioned our failed first women's meeting in my last letter, but Arinor and I have made progress on planning the second. I have invited a few acquaintances, but I'm not sure if any of them will come. Most of my closest friends don't live in Plymouth, and travel is difficult at this time of year. Even if they could travel, I'm not sure they would. Not every husband is as supportive of his wife speaking her mind and engaging in political pursuits as you. I think it possible a few of Arinor's contacts may attend, though. She has made quite the impression in the short time she has been here. We tried to impress upon everyone invited that nothing radical would be happening at this first meeting. We simply want to get to know other like-minded women and share ideas in a safe space. I think several women have found that concept appealing.

Our boys keep me endlessly busy during the day, of course. They miss you dearly too and are counting the days (quite literally in George's case) until your return. You'll never believe it, but at night, when I can't sleep, I have started writing a play! Do you remember when I used to write those, before we had children? I mentioned this to Arinor, and she asked what I would write about if I wrote a play now. My mind immediately raced through all the possibilities, and I landed on something I'm quite excited about. I won't reveal it all now, except to say I am having so much fun writing the villain based on a certain governor who absolutely deserves the role I have cast him in...

I do miss you, Sam. I grow so tired of talking and waiting, mincing words instead of acting. I want to do something. Perhaps I grow more reckless the more I miss you, but the political gatherings I host just don't feel like enough anymore. There is a Patriot rally in the new year, just over three weeks from now, and I wish to attend. I think I might, with Arinor. She thinks it's risky, but don't the greatest rewards come from taking a little risk? You risk unhappiness with your chosen spouse when you marry. You risk serious health complications or even death for mother or child when you have children. You risk your reputation, livelihood, security, and even life for freedom, for the hope of a better tomorrow, for yourself, your children, and future generations. Maybe life has presented me with this risk because it's one I need to take. What do you think?

Your ever-fixèd mark,
Clemency

Seven

C *lack-clack-clack.*

Clemency tapped her heel on the wooden floor, rubbing the lace of her sleeve between her finger and thumb with one hand and fanning herself vigorously with the other despite the thick flakes swirling past the windows. Her white cat, Moonbeam, snaked around her legs, rubbing against her ankles, but she ignored her demand for attention. Clemency's anxious mind only had room to concentrate on one thing right now.

"The snow has probably delayed them," said Arínor, watching Clemency fidget with a little too much pity clouding her grey eyes. "Maybe none of them will even be able to make it here in this."

"*You* did," Clemency pointed out.

"Not everyone has my tenacity," said Arínor.

"You mean insanity," Clemency's nine-year-old son, Charles, called from behind the open book propped on his knees. He lounged on the sofa at the far end of the room.

Clemency frowned at her middle child. "I thought you were going to play in the snow with your brothers during our meeting."

"What meeting? I only see Arínor. No point in freezing to death for someone who's always here."

"I'm not *always* here," Arínor protested.

Charles ignored her and continued reading.

A loud knock echoed in the snowy silence.

Scrambling to her feet, Clemency shooed Charles out of the room and turned to watch the doorway, heart pounding.

Thompson came in with a woman bundled in a fur cloak, her stiff bonnet lined with a layer of lacy snowflakes.

"Hannah!" Arínor exclaimed, hurrying over to hug the newcomer.

Teeth clenching, Clemency tried to slacken her taut stomach. She hadn't realized Arínor had become close enough with any of her new Plymouth friends to greet them with something as intimate as a hug. Arínor didn't even greet Clemency that way.

Thompson only had time to help Hannah remove her snow-laden hat and cloak before another sharp rap echoed down the hall. A minute later Thompson reappeared with a younger woman, wearing glasses, her hands buried in a muff. She declined Thompson's offer to take it with her cloak.

"Miss Richardson—Charlotte—I'm so glad you were able to make it," said Arínor, beaming. "Charlotte, Hannah, this is my friend Mrs. Warner."

"Welcome to my home," said Clemency, gesturing for them to take a seat on the sofas. "And please, call me Clemency. Can I pour you some coffee or chocolate?"

Once everyone had a warm beverage cupped in her hands, Clemency said, "Well, it's wonderful to see other women interested in sharing ideas and expressing their opinions. I know it's hard to have a voice, or to use it to speak too loudly, but we think it's so important for our voices not to get lost or be forgotten."

Silence and side glances greeted her little welcome speech, and Clemency wet her suddenly dry lips. Perhaps she had started too boldly despite her deliberately less aggressive word choices. "D-do you feel that way too?"

Hannah and Charlotte stared intently into their cups, Charlotte with a little furrow between her brows. Clemency glanced at Arínor, who offered her a small, sad smile and a shrug, as though she had expected no less.

"I met Charlotte on a house call to assist her bedridden mother," Arínor offered cheerfully to fill the awkward pause. "The doctor asked me to fetch Charlotte's father, Mr. William Richardson, after he had examined her mother. I tried the library, thinking he might have decided to pass the time by reading, but instead found Charlotte wedged in the corner behind a chair with her nose in a book. Her father doesn't believe women need to learn how to read, so she taught herself, and still must sneak into the library in stolen moments when her father's distracted if she wants to read."

A squeak of sympathy escaped Hannah's lips, and Clemency tilted her head and raised her brows in admiration. "An impressive feat," she said.

"Not that impressive." Charlotte shrugged, though twin roses bloomed on her cheeks. "I lose my nerve a little when he goes on one of his puritanical rants about women reading being akin to witchcraft, but he's away for work a lot, so it's not always that difficult."

"Witchcraft?" echoed Arínor.

"Yes. He inherited his father's fear of witches and magic," explained Charlotte, rolling her eyes. "Thinks women learning to read opens more doors for them to tempt the Devil through and lure others to sin."

"Well, he sounds like a delight to live with," said Arínor.

Charlotte snorted. "Unfortunately, he's not the only one who inherited a fear of the unknown around here. There's more lingering anti-witch sentiment than you'd think."

"Which makes your determination to learn to read and not miss out on something just because you're a woman all the more impressive," said Hannah. "I wish I were more like that. Maybe I can be, now..."

Her voice quivered with uncertainty, though her tawny eyes glowed with gratitude toward Arínor.

"Hannah is recovering from some chronic pain Molly and I recently helped her with," explained Arínor. "She didn't have a great experience with the doctor. He kept dismissing the severity of her pain as a woman's sensitivity, claiming women had a low tolerance for pain."

Clemency snorted. "I'd like to see how high Doctor Arnold's tolerance for pain is if he, say, had to give birth. I'm glad you're feeling better, Hannah. I've heard Arínor's remedies can work wonders."

"Almost like magic," agreed Hannah.

Skirts rustling a little as she shifted in her seat, Arínor unlatched her gaze from Hannah's and dropped it to her coffee. "Yes, well. We all have our different skill sets. Clemency is a fantastic writer. I've read some of her pieces on King George and the British taxation policies. They're delightfully scathing."

"Oh?" said Charlotte, straightening and setting down her coffee with interest. "Could I read one?"

"Arínor's kind, but I just write them for my own amusement, really," replied Clemency churlishly.

"Oh, do let us read one. I could use a good laugh," said Hannah, leaning forward, her face alight with curiosity.

Arínor raised an eyebrow at Clemency. Here was the interest they had hoped for, a chance to show these women they weren't just here for gossip. It was not how she had intended the meeting to go, talking of flawed British policies and the dangers they posed to a peaceful, functional colony instead of women's rights, but if they liked it and respected her opinions instead of dismissing them as an ignorant woman's drivel...

"Well, all right then," conceded Clemency, and she bustled over to her desk in the next room to retrieve one of the pieces Arínor had referenced.

Excitement buzzed in the air between them once Hannah and Charlotte had both had a chance to read it, invigorating and electrifying. They praised her wit and intellect, insisting the insights were unique and astute enough that she should submit it to a newspaper for publication.

"But I'm a woman," protested Clemency without thinking, the response automatic.

Arínor slapped a hand over her own face. "Isn't that what we're doing here? Challenging conceptions of what a woman can and cannot do? Even if they reject you, even if they dismiss it before reading it, simply because it was written by a woman, at least they'll see a woman is interested in politics and has the gall to do something about it."

"It would be so brave, and inspiring," said Hannah.

"Change has to start somewhere," said Charlotte.

Clemency surveyed the wide-eyed faces leaning toward her like a wave drawn to the shore. A small smile tugged at the corners of her lips, widening slowly like a long-locked door creaking open.

"I guess it's time to see if the quill is indeed sharper than the sword."

January 17, 1770

Dear Mrs. Warner,

> *We regret to inform you that we are unable to publish your political piece entitled "Taxation Tensions", as we only accept writing from male authors.*
> *Sincerely,*

Matthew Hankle
Editor, Boston Gazette

Brushing the feather of her quill across the splotched ink of the letter that had arrived an hour ago with a plump snowflake melting into the folded creases, Clemency read the phrase *only accept writing from male authors* over and over until her vision blurred and a hollow ache gnawed at her stomach. She had known this would be the most likely outcome. Arínor had known it. She tried to hold on to Arínor's words, remind herself that even submitting it had been an act of resistance, one that had inspired other women, and hadn't that been the point?

But it still stung, carving out a festering wound that was infected and oozing. Even after it scabbed over, she knew it would itch and burn. Her first rejection as a writer. The late nights of perfecting every word choice, crafting sentences as sharp and witty as a rapier, distant with her children, though physically present, as she had obsessed over whether her commentary was too radical or not radical enough. All for nothing. Dismissed without a second thought, not because her writing had been bad but because the physical anatomy she had been born with automatically disqualified her. All the labels associated with her gender branded her as not worthy. Woman. Unintelligent. Uneducated. Unqualified. Undeserving. Unworthy.

Not enough.

She had decided to join the Patriot rally tomorrow night, excited to make a statement with Arínor by probably being the only women in attendance. Now she despaired of the idea. What was the point?

When a knock sounded at the door, Clemency flinched. Her shoulders hunched lower. For the first time since meeting her in Boston, Clemency hoped it wasn't Arínor. She didn't think she could face her right now.

Thompson escorted Clemency's neighbour and friend Sarah Aldridge into the dim room. Only now, when she had to squint to see the concern knitting Sarah's eyebrows together, did she realize she had forgotten to light more candles against the onslaught of dusk.

"Is everything all right?" Clemency asked Sarah, rolling her shoulders back to sit up straight, disturbed by Sarah's anxious eyes and wringing hands. Her mind jumped to the pallid, sickly face of Sarah's older husband when she had seen him a week ago. "Is Mr. Aldridge well?"

"He's recovering well, yes, though it was a nasty flu," replied Sarah. "I'm not here about Cyrus, though. I wanted to tell you..."

Sarah glanced at Thompson.

Taking the hint, Thompson turned and left them alone.

"I wanted to warn you, actually," Sarah started again.

"Warn me? Goodness, that sounds dire," joked Clemency. "Did the boys get into trouble again?"

Rubbing her crestfallen face with her hands, Sarah blurted from between her fingers, "It's you, Clemency. There have been rumours about you and that women's meeting you hosted. Started, I think, by one of the women you invited who didn't come. I came to warn you that some folk are calling this radicalization of women... well, they're calling it witchcraft."

Clemency swayed a little where she sat, her vision blurring again.

"Witchcraft?" she repeated, the word so foreign on her numb tongue she slurred it a little. "But that's absurd. There's nothing even remotely magical or demonic about a few women meeting to discuss our place in the world."

"I know. I admire what you're doing, but... I just wanted to let you know what people are saying. They say talk can lead to action, and when women act together in defiance of God's will, they may burn in the Devil's inferno—and pull others in to burn with them." Sarah expelled this last sentence in a rush, as though terrified of voicing it aloud but determined to repeat it verbatim so Clemency could understand the severity of the rumours.

"Well, of all the puritanical nonsense..." Clemency fumed, words failing her. "Thank you for warning me, Sarah. I shall take it into consideration."

Sarah sighed in relief. "That is all I ask."

She took her leave, and Clemency stared at the candle on her desk, watching the flame flicker and cast fitful shadows on the wall. Her erratic heartbeat kept time with the shadows' jolting dance. Moonbeam leapt onto her desk and rubbed her chin against Clemency's fingers, purring. Relenting, Clemency scratched her jaw with one hand and flattened the raised hairs on the back of her neck with the other.

Rumours of witchcraft elicited shivers down her spine. Salem, Ipswich, Andover—all were close enough to Boston that those fateful trials more than seventy-five years ago still lived in the memories of her acquaintances' parents and grandparents. But accusations of witchcraft were not as rampant or taken seriously anymore. If a few next-generation Puritans thought her politically inclined actions in alignment with the Devil just because she was a woman, so be it. She would not yield to their unfounded fear.

And she would not be deterred by one rejection either. She just had to alter her approach.

Maybe the quill wasn't as sharp or instantly fatal as the sword, but it could cut deeper.

She would go to that rally and report her observations. She would take precautions to protect her family and their reputation, but she was done letting others' fear dictate her actions.

"This binding is itchy," complained Arínor, gripping the chest wrap beneath her waistcoat and adjusting it yet again.

"Stop adjusting it, or you'll give us away!" hissed Clemency, pulling her hat a bit lower down on her forehead. Unsure what to do with her frigid, bloodless hands, she ran them over the brass buttons of her coat, eventually settling on gripping the edges in her fists.

"You look ridiculous." Arínor sniggered, shivering beneath her cloak.

"Yes, and you look perfectly natural tugging at your cravat like that," Clemency retorted dryly, watching Arínor struggle with the knot of white fabric beneath her cloak's clasp.

"I think it's these clothes that are unnatural," said Arínor, pulling at the tight breeches around her hips. "Tight, impractical, and foppish. I thought men's clothes would be more comfortable. *Less* restricting."

"Shh!" admonished Clemency with a wave of her hand as a man in front of them looked over his shoulder with narrowed eyes.

A crowd had gathered at the rally site in the town square, forming a semi-circle in the snow around a man standing on a precarious stack of wooden crates. Clemency and Arínor had joined the back of the crowd, Arínor glancing at Clemency out of the corner of her eye every few minutes.

"You'll get a crick in your neck," Clemency muttered through gritted teeth.

"Better than a knife in my back," Arínor retorted, but she relented and trained her eyes on the speaker for a bit.

Clemency appreciated her friend's concern, but she felt like an impetuous child in need of a watchful nanny. Her husband's letter this morning had put her in a fickle mood, not a fey one. She understood the wisdom in his suggestion that perhaps the time was not quite right for a women's rights revolution—the colonies could only handle one revolution at a time, and they must win freedom and independence for all before women could win freedom.

Humbled and excited for his upcoming return, Clemency had thrown herself into plans for the rally with notable renewed vigour. He had thought the rally a good idea in principle if it was indeed peaceful, though he did caution her to be aware of the crowd's mood and had pointed out that there was an increased risk of her attending as a woman.

Which was why she had decided to attend dressed as a man.

Though Arínor had advised against coming, claiming she could see a reckless fire burning in Clemency's eyes that unnerved her, Clemency had insisted she would come whether Arínor accompanied her or not. Grumbling, Arínor had reluctantly agreed to join her, but Clemency knew it was partly to ensure her supposedly reckless mood didn't get her into trouble.

But taking calculated risks was not the same as being reckless. No one in her household knew she was here. She had told Thompson and their nanny and maid, Mary, she was going to Arínor's for the evening and had tucked her children into bed dressed in one of her normal gowns. Molly was out at an overnight call, so they had changed at Arínor's, and Clemency would change back before returning to her house. No one had seen them leave, and she would make sure no one observed their return. This was a rally, a peaceful gathering in support of Patriot ideals, not a formal protest or attack on Loyalists.

Arínor still eyed her uneasily, as though afraid she might disturb the peace and create danger. Clemency scowled and directed her attention to the man spouting Patriot ideals like a fountain.

"No taxation without representation!" he cried, shoving his fist into the air.

The crowd raised their fists, and Clemency punched hers into the air along with them, her breath misting the cold air as she shouted, "No taxation without representation!"

After a brief hesitation, Arínor shrugged and pumped her fist too, echoing the refrain.

Veins vibrating with exhilaration, Clemency shouted along with the crowd, not even bothering to deepen her voice, knowing hers was just one among many, lost to the chorused cacophony. Her heart soared in her weightless chest, alive with the flight of freedom.

Pain stabbed her foot, crushed by the man in front of her stumbling a step back as the crowd jostled a little. She cried out and bent to grab her foot, her hat falling off.

"I'm so sorry, sir. Let me grab that for you," said the man, turning to pick up Clemency's snow-dusted hat. He looked up to give it to her and paused, the hat hooked loosely in his limp hand. He tilted his head, peering more closely at Clemency's features, and she turned her head, lifting her collar to hide her face a little, heart racing. Eyes widening in her peripheral vision, he opened his mouth—and Arínor blew a handful of minuscule stars from nothingness into his face.

Clemency's breath froze in her lungs.

"Look, fireflies!" Arínor exclaimed, distracting him.

The man swatted the swarming stars out of his face, and Clemency snatched her hat from his hand, then turned on her heel and vanished into the crowd. A second later Arínor appeared at her side, and they dodged and weaved through bodies until they pushed through the back of the crowd on the other side of the semicircle—and ran.

Eight

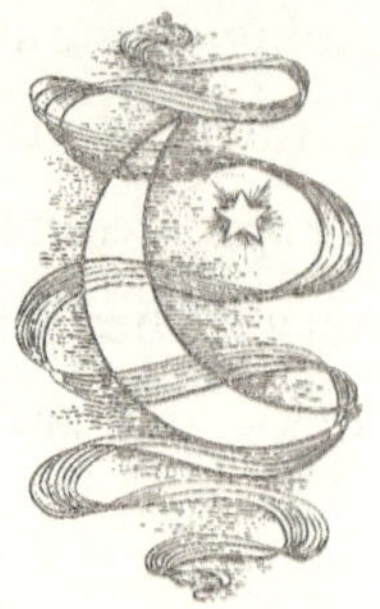

Vermilion flames licked the ebony sky, tasting the stars. Arínor basked in the heat of the bonfire they'd started on a dry stone platform cleared of snow behind Molly's house in celebration of their first successful rally, thawing her frozen toes, though the stone bench beneath her thin breeches numbed her rear. Clemency had changed right away when they had gotten back to Molly's, but Arínor had just thrown a heavy wool cloak over her men's clothes to hide the evidence and let her hair down. She sidled a little closer to Clemency under the pretense of needing the extra body heat, taking a swig from her bottle of cider.

"God, what a rush!" Clemency exclaimed, throwing her head back and barking a laugh. She whooped and crowed, howling her excess energy to the moon. Her mottled cheeks gleamed in the firelight, thawing unevenly, and she held one hand out to the flames, the other lifting a bottle of wine to her pale lips.

Arínor laughed, her grin so wide it cracked her chapped lips. She had never seen Clemency this wild and untamed, free of societal restraints and gender conformity. Strands of hair escaped the black ribbon tying it at the base of her neck, some plastering across her forehead, some framing her face. Arínor longed to tuck one behind her ear.

"Do you think that man recognized me?" Clemency asked, chewing her lip.

"I think he *thought* he did, but I'm sure he will just assume he was too drunk after you suddenly vanished," Arínor reassured her.

"Hopefully." Clemency's voice was calm, even as she added, "He'd have to be drunk to believe those stars were actually fireflies in January."

Arínor's heart stuttered, and her breath hitched, caught on the lie that immediately tried to escape her lips. Clemency's unflinching eyes bored into hers, hooking her attention with unyielding intensity, and in that moment, Arínor realized Clemency had guessed the truth and would not be satisfied by anything but an admission. Swallowing past the barbed misgivings of her dried throat, Arínor opened her mouth, then paused, the words sticking to her tongue. She wanted to share this secret with Clemency, share who she was at her core, bare her full self to her, but terror seized her throat and squeezed. If Clemency didn't accept her magic, if she denounced her as a friend or decried her as a menace, she would have to start over again. Flee the Province of Massachusetts Bay and find somewhere else to live on Earth or return to Arwé and face Vashi.

Focusing on the firelight glint in Clemency's cobalt-blue eyes, Arínor choked out, "No, those weren't fireflies. I've never even seen a firefly. I've just heard Molly talk about them sprinkling the night sky in summer like twinkling stars. Those were stars. Well, more specifically they were dust motes enchanted with starlight that I summoned with Celestial magic. I... I have magic."

Clemency's eyes widened with each word, and her lips slackened as she whispered, "I knew it."

Even through the palpitations of her heart and the terror numbing her brain, Arínor imagined tracing a finger lightly along Clemency's parted lips. She leaned a little closer.

"Who *are* you?" Clemency breathed, so close their puffed breaths intertwined, mingling in the space between them.

Arínor thought she saw Clemency's gaze flicker to her lips, and heat swooped low in her belly—but then she was leaning back, turning her face to gaze into the dancing flames, and downing another gulp of wine.

Arínor tipped more cider into her mouth and swallowed the kiss poised on her lips, shifting her gaze to the fire. It was difficult to know where to begin. Though she knew it would be overwhelming, she also knew building trust was imperative if she hoped to keep Clemency in her life, and that meant baring it all. No lies. No omissions.

"I guess I'm the closest thing to a witch you have in your world, though that's not what magic folk are called in mine," Arínor started. "I'm from a world called Arwé, a parallel sister world to Earth, accessed through portals."

Clemency's crestfallen face sliced a gash across Arínor's heart. "I thought you were about to tell me the truth."

"I *am* telling you the truth. Women are respected and equal to men where I'm from because it's a different world, not just a different region of Earth. I know it must seem impossible, but sometimes the impossible is the only logical explanation. And if you can believe in magic, why not other worlds?"

Clemency's clenched lips suggested skepticism still punctured her willingness to further suspend disbelief, but she didn't argue, so Arínor continued her explanation. "I'm an Armindí. The Armindí are a largely nomadic race of immortal beings evolved from lightning birds. I'm also a shape-shifter, one of the rare few of my race still gifted with the ability to turn into a lightning bird. And I have Celestial magic, a branch of magic encompassing Sun, Moon, Star, and Void magic."

Clemency's eyes enlarged with each new revelation, her awe at the potential existence of such wonders making Arínor more self-aware of her own attributes.

"Everything I've told you about myself before you knew I had magic is also true. I'm skilled with herbal medicine, and a healer at heart. I specialize in helping women with their specific medical needs. I work at an apothecary in Boston and will have to return there soon. I have no spouse, and I left my family behind when I came to Earth. I miss them every day. And I am so grateful to have met you, Clemency," Arínor finished, daring to glance at her friend.

Tears glistened in Clemency's eyes, and Arínor's heart slammed into her rib cage. Tears of joy... or sorrow?

"Do you hate me?" Arínor asked when she could stand the silence no longer.

"Hate you? Of course I don't hate you," said Clemency, and she chuckled through her tears. Relief that Clemency appeared to believe these fantastical claims despite her skepticism seeped through Arínor's veins. "These are tears of wonder that magic exists, of gratitude that you trusted me with your secret—and a little of envy."

That last surprised Arínor, and she chugged more cider to hide her confusion. No one had ever been envious of her before, except maybe her nephew Kat, but that was because he wanted to fly like a lightning bird. "Why envy?"

"Well, if I had magic, I could make sure my husband didn't have to work and be away all the time. I could make things better for women, more equal and fairer. I could free the colonies from British rule without anyone having to suffer, and bring prosperity and good health to everyone."

Warmth welled in Arínor's chest and pooled in her veins, spreading throughout her whole body. Not once in that list of wishes had Clemency asked for Arínor to grant them for her, to use her magic on her behalf or suggest that Arínor owed it to her. She was her friend without expectation or ultimatum and needed no compensation for that besides a friendship reciprocated.

"You know, that's not how magic works," Arínor clarified, hugging her knees to her chest. "I can't do any of those things. But it's a nice idea."

They stared into the flames, feeding them their troubles, leaving behind only the sparks of ideas, the pops and crackles of profound conversation.

"I'm glad we were able to do this tonight," said Clemency after a few minutes. "Sampson is coming home soon, and I think I might need to take a step back. Adopt a more focused approach to radicalism."

Arínor slowly lowered the bottle of cider. Her husband would be in Plymouth soon?

Though he seemed a nice man and a supportive husband from everything Clemency had told her, Arínor's stomach knotted at the idea of meeting him. She knew Clemency was married, knew she loved her husband—but she also knew love could change. It could fade, morph into like or lust, end and start anew with another. Love could be platonic, familial, friendly. She could love Sampson and be falling in love with Arínor. Lately she had thought Clemency's definition of love could be changing. The way she looked at Arínor sometimes, or the way their hands brushed, or breaths mingled... as though a longing lurked just below the mask of propriety, unspoken but passionate.

"What will he think of us?"

Clemency scrutinized Arínor's carefully neutral face, eyebrows drawing together. "What do you mean? What's there to think? You're a dear friend to me, and a partner in political schemes. You may tease a more daring side out of me, encouraging me to stay true to myself like a sister would, but there's nothing untoward or improper about that. I'm sure he'll be thrilled to finally meet you after all the times I've mentioned you in my letters."

The door to Arínor's heart slammed shut. Her breathing became shallow.

Clemency did not reciprocate her love. Not in the way she had hoped.

She had formed a sisterhood, not a romance. Maybe she was fated to only ever have unrequited love.

"So, you're taking a step back from fighting for women because of your husband, to make sure you toe the line of a good wife and mother," said Arínor, not bothering to hide the bitterness coating her tongue.

Clemency's whole body turned to Arínor, fixing her with her full attention. "I always try to toe that line. There's nothing wrong with wanting to be feminine. I can be feminine and have a mind of my own. My causes are important to me, but my family is everything. I would sacrifice anything for them."

"Your causes, or your husband's? Are your thoughts on taxation and independence for the colonies your own, or regurgitations of your husband's?"

"How dare you—"

"You sit up there on your moral high ground, waiting for the socially acceptable compass to point you in the right direction, but life is not a map that can be navigated," Arínor plunged on, cutting Clemency off. "There's no one right answer, because the question is always changing, and even the same question can have a different answer each time you ask it. What your husband thinks is right today may be wrong tomorrow and may always be wrong for *you*. It's not enough to care about a cause if you can't fight for your own freedom first!"

Arínor regretted her words as soon as she had said them, but before she could take them back or apologize, Clemency had leapt to her feet, shouting, "How could you even suggest my writings are just thinly veiled plagiarism, accusing me of every flaw men think defines women? What happened to sisterhood, to lifting each other up instead of helping men tear us down? You accuse me of not taking a stand, but what about you? Women are treated well in your world. That's my crusade, not yours. So, what do *you* fight for, Arínor?"

"I..."

But Arínor could think of nothing.

"You fight for nothing, because you're too afraid of falling!" exclaimed Clemency, answering her own question. "So you run instead. You ran away from whatever problems plagued you in your world, hiding behind self-deprecation to mask your self-loathing instead of facing your regrets. What are you so afraid to face?"

Screams of terror, panicked pleas, angry jeers and shouts, torches, fire—they all flooded Arínor's mind, drowning her senses and blurring her vision. Her entire body shook, fighting her decision to divulge her past, but she steeled herself, taking a deep breath and bracing for the pain. It was time.

"I had a... friend, once. Elandra," said Arínor in a low voice, her old partner's name sticking to her tongue from disuse. She didn't think now was the time to explain to Clemency that she had romantic relationships with women, if Clemency hadn't already picked up on Arínor's feelings for her. The change in Arínor's tone placated Clemency, and the red receded from her cheeks as she lowered herself back onto the bench beside Arínor.

"Among the Armindí, your inaugural trek is a huge milestone. It signifies maturity, a ceremonial embracing of a non-linear life, wandering the road less travelled, knowing life has a way of showing you what you need, when you need it. I was nineteen when I embarked on my first nomadic journey without my parents, travelling to a town in Déluren to sell my family's remedies with Elandra. We arrived without incident, and in between customers at our first market, I entertained Elandra by sending spots of stardust swirling around her, then vanishing them through a void. It was just innocent, silly fun."

Arínor forced a swallow past the serrated lump in her burning throat.

"That night, we camped in our wagon on the outskirts of town," Arínor continued in a hushed voice, dredging up the words like crumbling clods of waterlogged dirt. "We were already asleep when a mob of angry townsfolk attacked our camp, shouting about the evils of Celestial magic. I haven't mentioned this yet, but it's feared in my world, associated with a man who uses it for heinous practices. I rushed outside to confront them, and they started throwing things at me. A few closed in and started punching and kicking. I fell and twisted my ankle. Fearing for my safety, Elandra rushed out and claimed it had been her Celestial magic, not mine. She told me to run. I didn't argue. I didn't insist it was mine to save her in return or try to use my Celestial magic to save us both. I was terrified, bleeding and injured. I couldn't think straight and just acted on instinct. Elandra had told me to run, so I fled. I looked over my shoulder as I ran, and all I could see was the fear in Elandra's eyes as they closed in on her. The panic."

Tears streamed down Arínor's face, and she let them fall. Clemency recoiled in horror, her own eyes watery, her hand covering her open mouth. Whether horror at Elandra's fate alone or horror at Arínor's cowardice as well, she couldn't tell. But the sour tang of disgust burning Arínor's tongue and curdling her stomach was all too familiar.

"You're right, Clemency. I am a coward," choked out Arínor through her sobs. "I always have been. I don't know if I could have saved Elandra that night, or if we both would have died. My magic was still new, still raw and untamed. I had only just started to discover its applications, to experiment with its limitations. I didn't know how to use it to attack, and I was scared to try. Scared I might make things worse, hurt myself or Elandra, accidentally sacrifice someone, like Vashi had been rumoured to do. I didn't even think of striking them down or attacking them as a lightning bird. My terror blocked anything to do with magic from my brain, and it was only once I had fled on foot for a full day that I remembered I could shape-shift into a lightning bird and fly the rest of the way home. But I *should* have tried. I loathe myself for not trying, and I run from my own selfish impulses."

"We all fear our own flaws," whispered Clemency.

"I'm sorry, Clemency," Arínor said, shaking her head. "I accused you of following your moral compass too closely, but the truth is I wish I had a compass to guide my morals by. I guess I'm still trying to figure out what they are. I was afraid of killing someone that night, afraid of what it might do to my mind and my soul. Could I live with killing people if it was to save someone I loved? If we had both died, would that sacrifice have been worth it? What if I had died instead of Elandra? Would Elandra have then forever regretted surviving me? Was the cost of my life a price I was willing to pay? I didn't know. I didn't have any answers. All I know is that in the moment, I cared more about my own life and the stability of my own soul than Elandra's, and I'll never be able to forgive myself for that. But I can try to atone for my mistakes. I'm trying to make braver decisions, protect what I value, and choose the right sacrifices. But I feel like I'm failing. I'm still not fighting for the right causes."

Clemency laid a gentle hand on top of Arínor's, and a comforting warmth tingled her numb fingertips.

"Maybe it's not about finding the right cause," Clemency suggested softly. "If you don't believe in something with your whole heart, then maybe it's not the right decision for you in that moment. But like you said, circumstances can change. A decision that's not right for you now can be right for you tomorrow. You don't need to seek a cause to prove your worth to yourself. When you find a cause worth fighting for, you'll make the right sacrifice without having to think about it."

"Maybe you're right about my circumstances now," said Arínor. "But it doesn't change my regrets from the past."

"Well, why try to change them?" Clemency asked, a small smile curving her lips. "Why do we try to erase regrets? Mistakes are integral to the human condition and to the cycle of progress. How do we evolve and better our circumstances if we don't first make mistakes to learn what *not* to do? We may even repeat the mistakes, continue to make the wrong decisions, but that doesn't mean they should be erased. When we regret, we learn what's most important to us. It's kind of like my philosophy on missing someone. Sometimes the absence of something, the regret of what could have been, illuminates what we value most and shapes our moral compass to help better guide us in the future."

The flames crackled and hummed, filling the silence following Clemency's advice, and Elandra's face surfaced in Arínor's mind—but she didn't push it away. She studied the curls of her chestnut hair, the slant of her high cheekbones, the laugh lines already forming at the corners of her oval eyes—eyes the exact blue shade of Tor Stella Lalíté. A silent tear trickled down her cheek. Clemency was right—Elandra did not deserve to be erased.

"You know, what I said before..." Arínor began, wiping the tear dangling from her chin and facing Clemency. "I know your ideas are your own, that your brilliant mind makes keen observations about human behavioural patterns in relation to political incidents that others miss. And there's nothing wrong with wanting to make your husband happy or having feminine sensibilities. Femininity is not a weakness, nor are 'weak' and 'gentle' synonyms. In fact, gentleness and kindness are strengths, so if that's what being feminine means to you, then those sensibilities will only strengthen the power of your intellect."

"Thank you, Arínor," said Clemency. "I appreciate you recognizing that."

"I was just trying to say that you have a voice of your own, a voice with important things to say," Arínor continued. "You seek freedom from British rule and oppressive restrictions for women, but you must first find the freedom within yourself. I know you believe in a higher power, a god—I never have. The closest thing we have to deities in Arwé are the Keepers, the first beings to evolve in my world, and I don't exactly worship them. But whether you want to call it fate or an act of your god, or your own intellect and determination, I think you have power to do good in your world. But that starts with knowing you have your own voice, separate from your politically prestigious friends and husband. A powerful voice capable of change on its own—but only you can decide to use that power, and how."

Clemency smiled and squeezed her hand. "I know, and your support has meant so much. I'm glad you chose to come through that portal."

A broad grin banished the ghosts of regrets haunting Arínor's lips, and she replied, "Me too."

Nine

January 27, 1770

Dear Sam,

I know you are coming home in a week. I'm not even sure if this letter will reach you in time, or if you'll cross paths on the road like two ships passing on a foggy night, but I like the connection I feel to you when I write these letters, and need that right now.

I'm excited for you to meet Arinor, though I think she's nervous to meet you. She doesn't know how you'll feel about our friendship, but I can't imagine why, unless she just thinks she's too outside societal norms for you to approve. We did have a pretty heated fight after the rally. (It went well, by the way! It remained peaceful, and we were safe.) I don't even remember how the fight started, but in the end, I think it has strengthened our friendship. We understand each other better now, and I feel renewed determination to pursue my passions. My heart is aflame, but my head has cooled.

I think I need to take a new approach to the women's meetings. I have forged good friendships with women who share my passion for being proactive instead of taking direction. But I think you may be right that perhaps the timing is not optimal for a crusade for women's rights.

One revolution at a time. That's my new mantra.

I see the new focus of our women's group being what women can do in these uncertain times to make a difference in what I'm starting to think is an inevitable revolutionary war. I'm excited to discuss these new possibilities at our next meeting, especially because I'm fairly certain we'll have some more women joining us this time. Assisting the Patriot agenda seems much more agreeable (and attainable) to women.

My play is coming along as well. I'm now writing Act Two, and I think you'll rather enjoy some of the choice dialogue between the Patriots and Loyalists. Did I mention that was the main conflict? It may all need to be revised, but I'm feeling confident about the insights and commentary coming alive through the characters, and I'm eager to hear what you think. James insists there must be duels and battles, that any play worth watching has at least one good swordfight in it, so I'm seeing what I can do to appease him (and all our sons, really, who whole-heartedly agree with him).

I also have a bit of good news! I swallowed my pride and submitted one of my political pieces anonymously. What matters is that the ideas get out there, rather than ensuring the public knows a woman wrote them. And it was published! You are now married to a published author. Isn't it thrilling?

I can't wait to see you, my darling.

Love,
Clemency

Ten

"I thought the pains had stopped," Arínor whispered, wincing as Hannah groaned.

"They had. She was doing wonderfully during her last two cycles. I don't think she had cramps at all during her first one after we gave her that mixture. But this time..." Molly shook her head ruefully. "The doctor isn't even sure if they're cramps. The location of the pain is different. Same area but deeper, like it's in her bones."

"Her bones?" Arínor repeated. "But... that doesn't make sense..."

Frowning, Arínor reached out to Hannah's supine form on the bed with her magic. Sure enough, she could feel an emptiness in Hannah's pelvic area, not as dark and decaying as the cramps she had fixed, but deeper.

She reeled, head spinning and ears ringing. How had this happened? It had seemed fine when she used her magic before, looked like it had healed. She had used Void magic to fill and create, not empty.

Unless...

The decaying edges of the dark splotch marring Hannah... she had emptied the hollow of the decay before filling and stitching it together. Could the Void magic have just continued to empty? Drawing in everything around it without end?

Quick, shallow breaths rattled her chest, and Arínor shuddered. What had she done?

"Will she be all right?" Arínor asked Dr. Arnold, voice tinged with barely suppressed panic. "Is there anything we can do to help?"

Straightening up from his examination, Dr. Arnold heaved an enormous sigh as he pushed himself onto his feet. He wiped his fogged glasses on his waistcoat before admitting, "I don't know. I'm not sure exactly what's ailing her yet. I don't think the bone is broken, but based on her reactions when I move her hips and legs, I do think it's an issue with the bone, not her organs. There's no fever, so I'm not sure it's an infection either... I just don't have enough information yet. We'll let her sleep, and I'll return in the morning."

"Very good, Doctor," said Molly brusquely, tucking the covers around Hannah's listless limbs. "Just let me know if you need us to prepare something. We'll be here to assist in any way we can."

"I'll see you both in the morning, then," said Dr. Arnold. "Get some rest."

Arínor nodded her assent but couldn't speak. She couldn't rest. She couldn't be alone with her thoughts right now, couldn't let the panic build up and bubble over. Though she had informed Clemency of her magic a month and a half ago, Arínor hadn't been able to discuss it much after Sampson's return home two weeks later. But she needed to try now.

"I'm going to Clemency's. I'll see you tonight," Arínor informed Molly.

With one last look at Hannah, Arínor donned her cloak and billowed out the door like a brewing storm cloud.

When she pounded on Clemency's door half an hour later, it was Sampson who answered.

"Hello, Arínor," Sampson said, his tone light and smile pleasant, even if it didn't quite reach his eyes.

"Oh. I thought Thompson would answer," said Arínor, averting her eyes.

"It's nice to see you too," chuckled Sampson, shaking his head. "Thompson's outside with Clemency and the boys, helping prepare for a snow picnic."

"A snow... picnic?" Arínor repeated. "How does that work?"

"Don't ask me. It was George's idea." Sampson shrugged. "But Clemency thought it a wonderful one on our last day in Plymouth, so here we are."

"Last day? But I thought you weren't leaving for Boston for another week."

"We weren't, but then—let's walk around the back together. This is silly talking on the doorstep. Clemency will want to discuss it with you too. Let me just don my cloak."

After settling his cloak about his shoulders and securing a hat on his head, Sampson closed the door and tramped through the snow alongside Arínor. Her stomach fluttered, and she wriggled her shoulders, unsettled.

"So, what did you think of our little gathering the other night?" Sampson asked as they walked.

"I think you have some very... colourful... friends," answered Arínor, keeping her eyes on the snow. "Colourful" would not have been her first choice of word, but she didn't want to offend Sampson. Despite her best efforts at warm civility, she knew her envy sometimes skewed her interactions with him. She could tell he didn't always know how to interact with her either. He was always ready with an easy smile, laughed at the right moments, and went beyond polite propriety to make sure she felt comfortable in their home.

But sometimes, when he didn't think she would notice, he would frown at the floor as Arínor made Clemency laugh, or clench his jaw if Clemency touched her arm, or slant his eyebrows in suspicion if Arínor whispered something to Clemency. Arínor couldn't decide if these subtle actions spoke of jealousy, protectiveness, or suspicion, but increasingly she felt the need to tread lightly around him. They weren't often alone. Arínor's tense muscles stiffened her walk, straining her steps. She took a deep breath under the pretense of breathing in the fresh, cool air, trying to relax and loosen her muscles to reduce her awkwardness.

Sampson chuckled, a congenial sound that somehow still irked Arínor. "Yes, the Sons of Liberty can be a bit intense. I don't always agree with their extremism, but one must admire their tenacity and dedication to Patriot ideals."

Their dedication to Patriot ideals had indeed been obvious and impressive, but Arínor hadn't liked the way they had talked down to her—and all women present—using simple words and short sentences as though dumbing down a complicated topic for an inattentive child. At least they had made an exception for Clemency, who had clearly proven her intelligence to them already.

"It was certainly an interesting evening. And a lovely one," Arínor added with a small smile, remembering Clemency's striking sapphire dress. Clemency had come alive that night, almost two weeks ago now, still ecstatic to be reunited with her husband and thrilled to host the Sons of Liberty in her home. She had flitted from conversation to conversation like a whirbird, vibrating with passionate enthusiasm, her eyes burning with an insatiable hunger. She had dropped pearls of wisdom and insightful observations like bread crumbs, leaving a trail of impressed faces in her wake. Seeing her in her element had warmed Arínor with glowing pride—until she had looked over and seen the twin expression of pride on Sampson's face, reminding her that Clemency was his, not hers.

"I'm glad you enjoyed it."

"Arínor!" Clemency exclaimed in delight as they rounded the corner. "Come join us!"

"We're having a snow picnic!" George announced in his high-pitched three-year-old squeal. "Henry's making the snow chocolate. Charles is making a snow entrée. Winslow is in charge of making snow plates. James and Thompson are building a snow table—and I'm making snow cakes!"

"Don't forget Mary and me!" Clemency cried, laughing as she gestured at Mary. "We're in charge of decor."

Clemency stuck a few icicles she had broken off from the house along the edges of the crude snow table James was shaping like the scalloped edges of a lace cloth, then stood back to survey the results.

"Hmm, still missing something... I know!"

She grabbed three more icicles of varying heights with her mittened hands and stuck them pointy tip up into the middle of the table. "There! Candlesticks!"

Sampson clapped his hands in glee. "Perfect!"

A collective shiver rippled around the group as a bitter breeze nipped their cheeks, but no one complained. Arínor guessed they hadn't been out here too long, and the picnic would probably be quite short, but no one wanted to break the magic quite yet.

"Sampson tells me you're leaving for Boston tomorrow," said Arínor.

"Yes. As you know, we hadn't intended to, but then—"

Clemency cut herself off, glancing at her children. Arínor's stomach clenched.

What has happened?

"Mary, can you help Winslow with that plate? Sampson, you'd better help James and Thompson with that table before James pulls a muscle in his back trying to dig out that snow. We'll be right back."

Sampson's gaze burned Arínor's back as she followed Clemency around the corner.

"What's going on?" Arínor asked her as soon as they were out of earshot.

"I guess you didn't hear," said Clemency. "A boy has been shot and killed in Boston by a customs officer trying to defend a Loyalist. He was only eleven."

A deeper, icy cold froze Arínor's stomach, expanding to her extremities, and she squeezed her eyes shut, thinking of Kat and Élí. Only a few years older than her nephews, and this boy had died for a cause he probably knew nothing about.

"How?"

"There was a protest outside a Loyalist's shop. Apparently, the Patriot crowd was getting too rowdy, and the customs officer feared for the Loyalist's life, so he fired into the crowd from the window of his house, overlooking the street. The boy was the unfortunate recipient of this shot. Such a tragedy," said Clemency, shaking her head.

"That's... awful," said Arínor, stating the obvious. She had no other words.

"It's despicable. Outrageous. And it has enraged a good many people. Our friend Samuel Adams is organizing a funeral for the boy with the Sons of Liberty. I don't think we'll make it to Boston in time to attend the funeral, but Sampson wants to try. He must get back to Boston immediately now anyway, to help deal with the aftermath of all this, so we're leaving tomorrow instead now."

"Understandable. And the children are still going with you, I presume?"

Clemency nodded. "I don't know how long we'll be in Boston this time, and we have a place we can stay just outside of Boston, so they'll be coming with us. Aren't you due back at the apothecary soon? Maybe you could accompany us on the journey!"

"No, that's all right. I'm going to ask Meredith for a few more weeks here," replied Arínor. "That's what I came to talk to you about. Hannah is ill again. Well, not ill, exactly, but she's in severe pain, and Doctor Arnold isn't sure what's causing it. I think it might be linked to the pain she was having before, but I don't think the herbal mixture Molly and I made for her will help this time."

Arínor paused, looking around to make sure they were alone—she trusted Clemency with her secret, but not Sampson, or Mary, or Thompson, or even the boys, for that matter—then added in a low voice, "Or my magic. At least not in the same way I told you I used it last time. I want to stay and make sure Hannah will be all right, and check up on my other patients. I used magic on a few, though none in the same way as Hannah, so I don't think there will be the same problem... but I need to check. I need to make sure."

"Of course you do. But be careful, and remember not to let on about your magic to anyone else," Clemency cautioned. "One of the Sons of Liberty told me the oddest thing at that gathering we had. He said he'd heard a rumour from someone in Plymouth that the Patriots used witchcraft."

Arínor's stomach dropped, her heart thrashing in her chest. "*What?*"

"It's just ridiculous rumours, the sort of fear-mongering propaganda the Loyalists would use to gain new followers, opening up old wounds to bleed out proven hysteria-inducing tactics."

"Or someone saw me at the rally," said Arínor, voicing a fear that had stewed at the back of her mind ever since Clemency had revealed she'd witnessed her magic.

"No one else saw you at the rally, trust me. The man just laughed it off," Clemency assured her. "But I've been thinking about that rally too. I know it was a peaceful gathering of people on the same side, and even Sampson thought it would be fine if we took precautions, but what if it had turned ugly? What if a Loyalist had been there and gotten upset, or the crowd had gotten too rowdy in their support? That could have been us dead. I could have left my children motherless. I was a fool to take such a risk."

"We were both fools. Maybe a bit of time apart will help clear our heads—introduce a bit of common sense back into our lives. I'll try not to miss you too much," teased Arínor with a wink.

Wrapping Arínor in a warm hug, Clemency smiled into her shoulder and said, "Stay safe."

When Arínor entered Hannah's house that evening, she found Molly curled against her patient like a cat, shielding her from the pain. The protective posture reminded her of both Gertie and her ma, and her heart ached for home so fiercely she pressed a fist to her chest to stifle the pain.

She tiptoed across the room and brushed Hannah's forehead with a feather-light touch. No fever. No beads of cold sweat. She breathed evenly, almost peacefully in her sleep, and for a moment, Arínor wondered if the doctor could have been wrong. Maybe the pain had just been from her cycle, and it had now passed.

But when Arínor closed her eyes and reached out with her magic, she could still see the growing void, feel it gnawing deeper. Taking a deep breath, Arínor plucked a strand of Void magic from her core and poured all her energy into it, every ounce of determination and vitality she could muster. With a steady precision, she filled and knitted together the gnawing hollow, careful not to let even the thought of emptying enter her mind.

Hannah shifted, curling closer into Molly, but did not wake.

There was nothing to do now but wait.

Wait, and hope that she had not killed her friend and first recipient of Void healing.

Eleven

Stoking the dying embers with a stick, Arínor hugged her knees with her other arm, her skirt fanning out on the stone bench. Though Molly kept this area as dry and clear of snow as possible so they could enjoy bonfires throughout the winter, the bitter wind had proven relentless tonight, and sooner than Arínor would have liked, the roaring flames subsided to murmuring flickers and finally dwindled to embers.

Maybe it was for the best. She had hoped the fire would burn away all thoughts, leaving her mind blank and numb, but her mind had betrayed her. Alone with her thoughts, Arínor had lost herself in flames reflecting memories of soaring over cloud-shrouded Vellé, peering out the wagon window to watch floating stars sharpen to bobbing torches, and smoke billowing from her room, violating her safe space. Though she could sit with these memories now without chasing them away, they still distracted her mind from the tranquility of sleep. And she needed sleep before having to face Hannah and her other patients—or victims—of Void healing.

But she didn't move. Poking at the embers satisfied a primal fascination to discover the line between life and death, experiment with its boundaries so she could be in control of her fate. Spread the embers too thin, break them up too much, and they died, snuffing out the final smouldering sparks. But stoke them just enough, give them the right angle to work with the elements instead of against them, and those smouldering sparks ignited into a new flame.

The smoke shifted slightly, folding against a gust of wind, or bending around an obstacle.

No breeze kissed Arínor's cheeks.

She sat up straighter, heart pounding, breath hitched. She unwound her arm from her knees, dropping her feet to the ground. The glowing embers flickered with pulsating heat, and thin tendrils of smoke spiralled into the air, but nothing else moved in the yard. No deeper shadows stirred beyond the firelight.

A resounding *crack* echoed in the still night air like the explosion of gunpowder from a musket.

She jumped, pulse now pounding in her throat, but it was just an ember exploding like a dying star.

Rein in your imagination, Arínor.

Shaking her head at her unnecessary jitters, Arínor stood up, stoking stick still in hand, and bent to throw some snow on the embers.

Once the fire had been extinguished, she retreated to the house, fixing her gaze straight ahead, ignoring the dark shapes shivering in the shadows. Snow crunched beneath her feet, and a few flakes floated down like ashes.

The back door yawned wide, creaking on its hinges.

Arínor froze. Her heartbeat thrashed in her ears like a caged animal, roaring to get out.

She had closed the door behind her when she had come out. Hadn't she? Had the wind blown it open?

A light flickered through the open doorway. The candle she had left burning in the kitchen was still lit, and she thought she could see the soft glow of another down the hall. Perhaps Molly had decided to come home instead of spending the night at Hannah's.

Stepping slowly, abandoning the pretense of nonchalance to swivel her head like an owl, Arínor crossed the threshold and entered the house.

An eerie silence greeted her, though Arínor chided herself that the silence shouldn't be eerie when it was expected. She *was* alone, after all. Slipping her finger through the candlestick holder's handle, she picked it up and proceeded down the hall toward the other soft glow.

"Molly?" she called into the silence as she walked.

No one answered.

She padded into the glowing drawing room and was deluged by darkness.

Blood rushed to her ears like the swell of a wave, drowning out all other sound.

"*Witch*," a voice hissed in her ear.

She screamed and whirled around, but no one was there.

"Wh-who's there?" she shouted, her voice shaking. "Show yourself!"

She tried to swallow, but her gummy saliva grated against her gritty throat.

A creak and a shuffle sounded behind her.

A *whoosh* of air snuffed the candle in her hand.

Her rapid breaths rattled in her ears like scraping bones. She seized a thread of Celestial magic from her core, though she didn't know—

A dagger scraped her throat, the flat of the blade pressing into her neck as the tip pricked the soft skin under her jawbone.

"*Witch!*" the voice hissed again in her ear, but this time she could smell the rum on the owner's hot breath.

She stamped her boot down hard on theirs, elbowed them in the gut, and threw her head back, unbalancing her attacker. The dagger dropped to the wooden floor with a clatter, lost to the darkness, but they didn't need it.

A rough hand seized the nape of her neck and slammed her into the wall.

Pain split her head, blood trickling from her ear as she crumpled to the floor. She rolled onto her back, moaning as she tried to see her attacker, but she couldn't make out more than a vague large shape in the darkness before it was on her again, reaching for her throat.

Her strangled scream gurgled as the salty tang of mixed sweat and snow dripped from her attacker's forehead down the back of her throat, making her gag. Thick fingers cocooned her neck and squeezed. She kicked out with her legs, but her attacker pinned them with their knees. She flailed her arms, trying to land a punch, but couldn't reach anything other than the strong arms crushing her throat. She thrashed, desperate to loosen the chokehold, landing increasingly weak blows wherever she could reach—but her vision blurred. Her feet twitched and spasmed. She summoned the storm cloud at the back of her mind, frantic to transform into a lightning bird, but she couldn't find it in the thick black fog sinking her brain into darkness...

Rage crackled through her veins like lightning, slicing through the dark fog.

Rage at those who manifested their fear of the unknown through vicious hatred.

Rage at those who indoctrinated the next generation to adopt their prejudiced fears.

Rage at those who elevated those fears to often fatal violence.

She would not die by the hands of an ignorant, mindless coward.

Light bloomed in her core. A burning star in a black void.

Seizing a strand of Void magic, she channelled it at her attacker and aimed for deprivation.

A whorl of black-and-silver magic radiated out of her hands and into her attacker's midriff, pummelling them off her and freeing her throat. Gasping for air, Arínor rolled herself up to a sitting position but kept her hands trained on her attacker, who she could now see was a man by the silver glint of her magic. A man she didn't recognize.

"Why are you trying to kill me?" she wailed.

Hunched around his midriff, his face contorted in pain, the man choked out, "Witch."

"But how did you know I had magic? I don't even know you."

"Rumours..." the man gasped.

"I've heard those rumours, and there has never been a name mentioned. Someone gave you a name, told you to come kill me. Who? *Who?*"

The whorl of her magic looped faster, coiling and spinning in tighter, intensifying circles.

The man screamed and threw his head back as a black shadow stained his stomach, its radius bubbling out like poisonous brew spilled from a cauldron.

"W-William Richards sent me to kill you," moaned the man.

William Richards? Charlotte's father? But how did he know...

A heavy dread suffocated her chest, cutting off her breath more effectively than her attacker's stranglehold, and sour bile burned the back of her throat, stinging her tongue.

Had Clemency betrayed her?

"And who told William Richards?" she forced herself to ask, needing to hear Clemency's betrayal confirmed.

"P-please, I-I don't know," the man choked out. "He said he'd come from a meeting. I don't know what about... He mentioned a name... I-I think he said... Sampson..."

Sampson.

Whether Clemency had told her husband Arínor had magic or he had falsely accused her of witchcraft to get rid of her, she didn't know. She didn't even know if he wanted her killed or just hoped that by spreading rumours, she would be disgraced in Clemency's social circles enough that she would no longer be welcome. All she knew was her rage swelled and intensified, electrifying her body and thundering through her mind. A wild, untamed rage, fractured from any semblance of restraint. A manic, vengeful rage.

Her attacker screamed, scrabbling at the gaping black hole expanding across his midriff, crawling up his chest, gnawing at his insides as it consumed him from within, sucking his entire being into its insatiable maw. His shrieks raised the hairs on the back of Arínor's neck and chilled her bones, but she did not relent.

She hadn't been strong enough to save Elandra by taking a life. She would be damned if she made the same mistake now and let someone take hers.

With one last blood-curdling shriek, her attacker vanished, lost to the void.

Arínor stood panting and staring at the empty space before her, trying, and failing, to calm the rage still coursing through her.

How could Sampson let his jealousy ruin his wife's friendship? She had known he was wary around her, seen the frowns and discomfort, but he had always supported Clemency, and even if Arínor had suspected jealousy, she hadn't thought him malicious.

Confusion swirled in her mind, melding and mixing the half-truths, dizzying her brain into a melting pot of accusations and acquittals until all thought evaporated, leaving only action.

Her core's white-gold light shone brighter than she had ever seen it, and she answered its beckoning call. Threading strands together, she created her own miniature full moon and held it aloft in her palm like a lantern. Its pearly glow illuminated the dagger on the floor, and she picked it up.

Magical moon light in one hand, dagger in the other, blank mind fuelled only by purposeful rage, she stalked out the door and into the snow.

Thick snowflakes floated down now, puffy and lazy, so when Arínor approached Clemency's home, she thought the dark windows signalled a slumbering household. The midnight hour must be nigh.

But then she spotted Sampson, his back to her, chopping wood by the front door—a task he would normally have a servant do.

Waiting to hear the results of the seed he planted, perhaps, Arínor thought. *Or distracting himself from his conscience's jeers and jibes on his moral character.*

She stalked toward him, padding silently in the fresh, soft snow, slinking like a shadow. A hunter closing in on her prey. Though she didn't need the full moon's magic glow to see by—the snow reflected its own soft light—she floated it above her palm still, keeping the connection to her magic. She didn't know if she would need the dagger or her magic and wanted to be ready with both.

Halting just out of reach of his swinging axe, Arínor raised the dagger—and paused.

She couldn't bring it down.

The fortress of her blank, purpose-fuelled mind crumbled, and the moat of morality and confusion flooded back in. Her blazing rage cooled, quenched by the icy glint of the dagger from her conjured moon light.

She may not have a moral compass, like Clemency, but she knew this was wrong. Rage and vengeance had consumed her, but this was not who she was. Killing in cold blood was not her. She used her Void magic for healing, for saving lives, not ending them. She wasn't Vashi.

She couldn't be.

Slowly she started lowering the dagger to her side, trying not to alert Sampson to her presence.

A terrified shriek pierced the snowy night.

"No!"

Clemency stood framed in the doorway, a wool shawl slipping off her shoulders from her heaving chest. She gaped at the dagger still half-poised to stab Sampson and the full-moon orb floating above Arínor's palm. Shock, horror, and hurt warred in her glistening eyes.

Sampson whirled, axe raised, ready to strike.

"Clemency, no. I wasn't going to—"

"Get away from my husband, witch!"

The moon light vanished, Arínor's connection to her magic breaking. She dropped the dagger in the snow and stumbled back, almost tripping over her cloak. *Witch.* Coming from Clemency's lips, the word was like a knife stabbed through her heart. Tears welled in her eyes, clumping with the snow and freezing her lashes.

"No..." she whispered. "No... he tried to get me killed..."

She lifted a shaking finger to Sampson, whose eyebrows shot up, wide eyes wreathed in genuine confusion. Arínor's stomach twisted. Had she really come to kill an innocent man?

Drenched in horror and shame, Arínor sprinted to the forest at the edge of Clemency's property, not daring to look back. She couldn't see the hurt in Clemency's eyes again, a hurt bordering too closely on hatred. Beneath the snow-laden trees, Arínor embraced the storm at the back of her mind and transformed into a lightning bird.

She launched off the ground and catapulted through the forest canopy, and Arínor soared away from Plymouth and into the darkness.

Twelve

M*arch 5, 1770*

Arinor,

~~*What were you thinking?*~~

~~*Are you safe?*~~

~~*Do you really want my husband dead?*~~

I don't know where to begin. I don't even know why I'm writing this. All evidence points to you trying to kill my husband without cause. The pain of that betrayal runs so deep, I know it is a scar I will bear forever. But I just can't shake the feeling that there's more to the story. I thought I knew you. I trusted you. The Arinor I knew was scared to take a life, so scared of what it would do to her soul that she wouldn't fight to save her friend. Concerned about morality, even if she didn't have all her own values and beliefs figured out yet. Did you stop caring about the fate of your soul? What has changed in the last month and a half since that bonfire after the rally?

Well, I'm not completely ignorant. I know at least part of what has changed, and that is Sampson coming home. Neither of you is as good at hiding your feelings as you think you are. I could feel the tension, see the looks (or deliberate avoidance). I know it must have been hard for you, having to suddenly share your best friend, and I know it was hard for Sampson to share the little time he gets with his wife with someone else. I tried to balance both, but I think I'm a little at fault too for not realizing how deep the friction ran. In my fervor to draw attention to political tensions, I ignored the tensions in my own home. I forgot how palpable fear of the unknown can be, and I lost control of my choices. For that, I'm sorry.

But a little jealous rivalry should not have been reason for murder.

You accused Sampson of trying to get you murdered, but I still can't figure out why. I've questioned Sampson about it since, of course, and he's baffled too. He swears he didn't try to get you killed, and I know I'm biased because he's my husband, but I'm not a simpering teenager at her first ball, blind to any flaws in her partner. I do believe he's telling the truth. He did admit to saying some less-than-favourable things about you to a few people, and he also admitted he wouldn't have minded if you had felt you couldn't attend as many social gatherings, because your reputation had been sullied—believe me, I gave him a good scolding about deliberately tarnishing someone's reputation, an unforgivable act in its own right—but he didn't want you killed. I think he's genuinely appalled at the very idea.

But I don't think you're lying. It just doesn't make sense for you to make that up. I believe you truly thought Sampson tried to have you killed, which means someone attacked you.

Right?

I'm so sorry if that's the case. I fear it all has something to do with witchcraft. That ridiculous warning from my neighbour, which I brushed off at the time. The stars at the rally. The bonfire. Maybe someone was watching us—you—closer than we knew. Sampson didn't say the words "witch" or "witchcraft" were involved in his unsavory speeches about you, but if he contributed to that narrative in any way, I am truly sorry. I know he would be sorry too.

And of course, I am so sorry for calling you a witch. I guess that's the real reason I'm writing this. I can't get it off my mind. The word taints my tongue, like a vile aftertaste that won't dissipate. Hurling that word at you was equivalent to hurling a spear at your heart. I do so want your forgiveness, but I'm not sure I'll ever be able to get it. A regret to add to my list, but one that I will hold close and never try to erase.

I'm not even sure if this is a letter I'll send, or if it will just end up as fuel for the fireplace. Even if I decide I want you to read it, I have no idea where to send it. To Molly back in Plymouth, maybe, or here in Boston, to Meredith at the apothecary. Maybe one of them will know where to get in touch with you. Or maybe you've left Massachusetts entirely. Maybe you—

"It's time to go, Clemency! You'll be late!" called Sampson from the foyer.

Clemency dropped her quill on the letter, blotting the last, unfinished sentence with a spray of ink, and hurried to grab her hat and cloak. Though James stood reservedly in the foyer, waiting to see his parents off, her other four children chased each other through all the adjoining rooms of the first floor. She snagged Winslow for a hug as he ran by, and nearly fell over trying to give Charles a kiss on the top of his head.

"Forget it, Clemency. You'll never wrangle them all here for a goodbye," said Sampson.

"Bye, boys! You be good for Mary!" Clemency called to George's retreating back as he chased his older brothers into the kitchen.

Sampson offered his arm as they stepped over the threshold. After a moment of hesitation, Clemency looped her arm through his, cognizant that they were still in sight of their children. It wouldn't do for them to worry.

Though she had almost joked about giving Sampson a scolding in her letter, in truth a new underlying tension had knotted between them. She did believe his side of the story—she had been married to him for fifteen years, and though she knew he could still evade or omit the truth, he had never been able to lie straight to her face, especially not for something this serious. But the trust between them had frayed. He had kept things from her, spoken ill of her best friend to their acquaintances behind her back, and most importantly, he had let his jealousy tarnish his trust in his wife. His trust in their love. He had doubted her love as an ever-fixèd mark, fearing the changes in her since she'd met Arínor, despite his show of support, instead of trusting that as she grew, her love for him would grow with her. Though she wasn't so immature or naive to think there were never doubts in a marriage, she had at least thought their love strong enough to transcend deliberate sabotage. Now she couldn't help but question the strength of his love for her.

After clambering into the awaiting carriage, Clemency checked the sapphire velvet drawstring pouch hanging from her wrist again, ensuring the clipping from her published article in the *Boston Gazette* and blank paper, quills, and ink bottle were intact. This would be the first women's meeting in Boston, the first meeting with the more focused vision of finding the niche women could fill in the pursuit of freedom for the colonies, and the first time she would take names to keep a record of attendance.

It would also be the first one without Arínor.

The saliva in her mouth still dried up at the idea of running a meeting alone, without the comfort of Arínor's quick laugh or confidence in the validity of women claiming power, but she knew she must show courage, even if she didn't feel it. As she'd shouted at Arínor after the rally, women's empowerment was her crusade. She needed to be able to fight it without Arínor.

As the carriage trundled through the streets, wending through pockets of shoppers and tradesmen, Clemency watched the silhouette of a bird soar against the setting sun, wild, free, and unburdened by plaguing guilt and frustration. She braced her fingertips against her aching temple, ignoring the slight crease between Sampson's brows in his otherwise carefully composed face that meant he was uncomfortable with the silence but didn't know how to break it. Perhaps it was ungracious of her, but she felt no qualms about letting him stew in his own guilt and uncertainty for a bit. Whether he had intended for Arínor to be killed or not, at least part of the blame lay on him for handling his petty jealousy poorly and not expressing his misgivings to his wife. She wouldn't instantly forgive to appease his pride.

As they drew closer to King Street and Town House, where the carriage would drop them off, raised voices filtered in through the open window. Craning her neck, Clemency spotted a small crowd gathered near the Custom House, but with the darkening sky, she couldn't see what they were raising their voices at. Across from her, Sampson frowned at the crowd, twisting his hat in his hands.

"I wonder what's going on there... Looks a little rowdy. Do you think maybe I should walk you over to the meeting? Or come into the building with you, perhaps?"

"There's no need. I don't even have to pass by them to get to Crooked Lane," replied Clemency, her tone a little more impatient than she had intended. "Besides, this is a women's meeting, meant for women to express themselves together in a safe space without men. If you come, however well intentioned your motives may be, it will set the wrong tone."

Sampson brushed the brim of his hat, ridding it of non-existent dust as he glanced at the crowd again, and Clemency sighed. She didn't have to punish him for benevolent chivalry, and if she was being honest with herself, his concern for her safety still warmed her chest like rich hot chocolate.

"Why don't you meet me outside the building when the meeting's over? And you can walk me back to the carriage instead of meeting in front of Town House again," Clemency offered.

Sampson's eyes brightened at the compromise, and his smile radiated impish innocence, like he was courting her again and had received her father's permission to escort her to a ball. It was an infectious smile she couldn't help but reciprocate.

Parting ways with Sampson's soft, chaste kiss lingering on her hand, Clemency strolled toward Crooked Lane. Though she didn't have to pass the crowd directly, she did draw near enough to spot a British soldier sur-rounded by almost a dozen men. The sentry didn't move, staring straight ahead with a white-knuckled grip on his musket as the men jeered and heckled, but his clenched jaw and throbbing neck vein suggested his pa-tience ebbed.

Clemency quickened her pace.

When she reached the white building of Sampson's old office, a few women already lingered outside, glancing nervously around the street at the passersby. She smiled a little at their obvious attempts at feigning nonchalance, their shared apprehension immediately calming Clemency's own nerves. She was not alone. The meeting hadn't even begun, and already she felt vindicated and seen.

"Sorry I'm late," said Clemency, startling one of the women, who hadn't seen her approach. "Shall we go inside?"

Producing a key Sampson had loaned her, Clemency unlocked the door and led them inside, lighting the candles. She blew dust off a peeling pine table, set the quill, ink bottle, and paper atop it, and placed herself on the side of the table opposite the other women, facing them. She pressed her fingertips into the tabletop to stop them shaking and took a deep breath, trying to dispel the nausea swirling in her stomach. Though only five women stood on the other side of the table, her weak knees trembled, and the speech she had rehearsed stuck to her tongue.

"Thank you all for coming," she said, her voice cracking a little. She cleared her throat and started again. "You are here because you care about the plight of the colonists and believe women have the strength and intellect to help the cause. But let's not pretend circumstances are different than they are. A woman's power is limited by law and by social construct, and we're not here to overtake political positions, take up arms, or brawl in the streets with British soldiers. We're not men, nor should we pretend to be."

A smattering of approving mutters rippled around the small group, and a few women nodded. Emboldened, Clemency rolled her shoulders back, straightened her posture, and continued.

"I used to think I had to choose what definition of a woman I wanted to be. Wife, mother, daughter, educated intellectual, feminine soul, opinionated citizen, political activist—I couldn't be all these things at once, and since societal expectations deemed some of these aspects of womanhood antithetical instead of synonymous, my choices would be dictated to me. But I was wrong."

The women exchanged skeptical glances, but a couple leaned forward a little.

"I want to show women that one day we can embody all definitions of womanhood if we start working toward that goal together. It won't be an easy path, or a short one, but even now we can start embracing multiple facets of womanhood, not by breaking societal rules but by playing them to our advantage."

"How?" asked Jane, one of the women she had told of the meeting personally. She rubbed her forehead. "Those are pretty words, but intention is not action."

"You're right," agreed Clemency. "Which is why I brought this."

She reached into her pouch, pulled out the clipping from the *Boston Gazette*, and held it up before smoothing it out on the table. The women all shuffled closer, leaning in to read the article.

"It's an anonymous article," observed another woman—one of Jane's friends, a woman whose name, Clemency thought, was Elizabeth—with a shrug. "Not exactly revolutionary."

Clemency let a self-satisfied smirk quirk her lips. "I wrote it."

All eyes locked on Clemency, ranging from astonished to excited.

"I wrote it and published it anonymously," Clemency explained, chest puffing up with pride. "I tried to publish it under my own name at first but was rejected because I'm a woman. I could have written under a pseudonym, adopting a man's name, but I chose to make it anonymous instead. I'm working on more articles right now, and a play, even, and hope to publish them all anonymously as well. I was able to share my opinions on our current political conditions, offer commentary on how I think it will unfold, and continue my duties as wife and mother. And this is just a start. Even small gestures can have a huge impact. We can cast the stones that send ripples of change across the colonies. Making a difference *is* possible as a woman. We just have to find our voice, empower other women to do the same, and find ways to circumvent the restrictions."

A volley of questions and comments was fired at her, ricocheting off one another.

"Where did you find the resources?"

"How did you find the time?"

"What did your husband think? Did you tell him?"

"Have any of your acquaintances figured out it was you?"

"How exactly did you submit the article?"

"What other ideas do you have?"

Clemency laughed, her mind buzzing, her chest weightless and breathless. Casting her gaze around to determine which question to answer first, she glanced out the window at the moonlit street beyond—and glimpsed a massive ebony bird perched on the roof of a building across the street, silhouetted against the star-strewn sky.

She had never seen a bird so enormous before. Larger than an eagle, it looked almost big enough to ride on, and its head appeared cocked in her direction. She mirrored the bird's head tilt, and the echoes of her laugh died abruptly, though she masked it with a dry cough.

Wrenching her gaze from the bird's, she refocused her attention on the women. "I would love to answer all your questions, and I will, but first I thought I might ask for your names, so I can record them on this paper. Don't worry—it's only for our eyes. Because women trying to help causes outside of charitable organizations is frowned upon, I do think we'll need to keep this group secret, at least at first. If the wrong person finds out we're fighting our own battle for the colonies, we could risk more than our reputations. So, before we proceed further, I need your consent, and your promise. Uplift your voice but protect each other."

Silence greeted this pronouncement, punctuated only by shifting feet and fidgeting fingers. Every woman exchanged a wary glance with another. Clemency's sweaty palms slipped on the slick table.

Finally Jane stepped forward. "You can write Jane Whittle down."

"And Elizabeth Averson," said Elizabeth, aligning herself with Jane.

The remaining three women consented to their names being written down as well, and Clemency added her name last, with a flourish.

"Maybe we can even give ourselves a name, like the Sons of Liberty," said Jane, eyes shining with excitement. "A secret name, of course, known only among the members."

"I like that idea," said Clemency.

"How about the Daughters of Freedom?" suggested Elizabeth.

"That's a good one," said Jane. "Or—"

A streak of forked lightning crackled and sizzled past the window, smiting the cobblestones just outside the door. Blinding white light pierced Clemency's eyes, and she threw up her hands to shield them. A few women screamed, and as the glow faded, Jane yanked open the door to get a better look.

"What the hell was that?" one of the women asked, clutching a shelf with a white-knuckled grip.

"I don't know. I don't even hear any thunder," said Jane. "And I just see snow."

Skin prickling, Clemency ran to the door and surveyed the street. Small snowflakes had started floating down to dust the hard-packed, icy layer of snow already coating the street. No one ran away or lurked in the shadows. The street was empty. Silent.

Clang, clang, clang.

A church bell pealed in the distance, a resounding series of gongs that reverberated down the street. And beneath the clangs, the din of roaring voices, swelling louder and louder. The swoop of Clemency's stomach spiralled a wave of nausea rippling up to her chest.

"Fire!" Elizabeth cried, eyes wide and frantic. "That bell means fire! We must go!"

"Yes, I think this would be a good place to adjourn tonight's meeting," agreed Clemency. "Thank you again for coming, everyone. Will you all be able to get home safely?"

They all nodded, bouncing on their toes and wringing their hands, clearly eager to be gone.

"Until next time, then," said Clemency, and they poured out of the door, stepping over the shattered cobblestones where the lightning had struck and scattering like ants caught invading a picnic.

Clemency surveyed the skies for a brewing storm or sign of more lightning but found only a crescent moon and starlight. Wrapping her cloak more tightly around herself to ward off the chill, she contemplated the street ahead, squinting to where Crooked Lane joined King Street. The noises came from that direction, louder with every tentative step she took toward them.

She knew she was supposed to wait for Sampson to escort her to the carriage, but he was nowhere in sight, and she didn't feel safe staying in the dark, empty street by herself, especially not with the threat of stray lightning strikes. Maybe a fire did ignite Boston, and she could help. She didn't want to take unnecessary risks, for her sake or her children's, but it couldn't hurt to at least see what was happening so she could make a more informed decision. If there was in fact a fire, Sampson may not even be able to get to her.

One peek around the corner at King Street told her it wasn't a fire.

It was a mob.

No longer the lone British sentry, the soldier she had seen heckled by colonists earlier had now been reinforced by seven additional soldiers—but the crowd must have been over fifty strong, with more joining every second. They shouted obscenities and threw snowballs and ice pellets at the soldiers, taunting and goading them into instigating violence, but though the soldiers held their muskets tipped with bayonets ready to fire, no shots rang out.

Boston's bubbling cauldron of rival tensions, bids for power, and desperate cries for freedom had boiled over, and people were about to get burned. *Macbeth*'s witches had brewed their potion to perfection, and now toil and trouble had been loosed upon the colonists.

Clemency scrambled to extract quill, paper, and ink from her pouch. If she couldn't join the fray and protest the unfair standards of British rule, she could at least report on it. She took a few steps into the street to better position herself as a witness.

"Clemency, stop!"

Her heart stuttered, tripping over its own beats in its race to accelerate. She knew that voice, but she didn't turn around immediately. She wasn't sure she was ready to face it.

A hand grabbed her wrist and spun her around.

Breathless, Clemency stared into Arínor's stormy grey eyes. All the questions she wanted to ask, the regrets she longed to apologize for, froze in her throat like fractals of ice.

"You must get out of here, Clemency. It's too dangerous. I've been watching them. There's no way those British soldiers will refrain from firing much longer," Arínor rambled, tugging on her arm.

"Arínor... what are you doing here?" Clemency asked, her voice hoarse as she ignored her friend's pleas.

"Look, I know you hate me, and I'm probably the last person you want to see right now, but you have to trust that I would never want you to be hurt."

"Never want me hurt?" Clemency repeated, the rising heat of anger thawing the ice in her throat. "How would attacking my husband not hurt me?"

"I know. There's no excuse for my behaviour, and I'm sorry. Even if he was behind the attack on my life, I should never have retaliated with more violence. That wouldn't have been fair to you or your children. But you're in danger. Now isn't the time to discuss this—"

"I'm not in danger. I'll be fine. I'm far enough back from the mob..." But she chewed her lip uncertainly as she glanced over her shoulder and realized the crowd had enlarged, and moved. The rear colonists were only a few feet away.

"Come on!" Arínor insisted, tugging Clemency's wrist again.

But Clemency dug her heels in, determined to voice two words: "I'm sorry."

Arínor's hand stiffened on her wrist, her whole body going rigid as she searched Clemency's eyes for a trace of mockery, her own eyes glistening wetly when she could find none.

"You don't need to apologize," said Arínor.

"But I do," insisted Clemency. "I ignored the tension I saw building between you and Sampson. I wanted everything and was willing to sacrifice nothing, and I called you a w-witch..."

Tears pooled in Clemency's eyes now too. Chest heaving with unreserved sobs, she let all the fear and anxiety, the extreme dichotomies of joy and sorrow, of wild rebellion and forced restraint pour forth. A release of emotion both cleansing and empowering.

Men swarmed from the direction of Town House toward Custom House, hurling insults and projectiles with equal temerity.

"Fire, damn you!" a voice bellowed from the crowd.

The colonists took up the goading chant, daring the British to kill them.

Clemency's sobs changed to desperate pants as her legs wobbled and ears rang.

"We have to go!" Clemency gasped, and she lurched a few steps away from the crowd.

But the mob swelled and receded like a cresting wave, sweeping Clemency up in its tumbling furl. Wrenched from Arínor's grip, she watched her friend snatch at the air and close her hand on emptiness.

"Clemency!" Arínor cried as Clemency was pushed and shoved deeper into the crowd, tripping and stumbling into people.

She saw Arínor shoving men aside, but more poured into the gaps, barricading her from Arínor's reach. Throwing her elbows out and jabbing anyone who came too close, Clemency fought against the tide pulling her away, screaming for the men to let her pass, but her voice was lost to the uninhibited, unhinged furor.

Shots popped and fizzled over the din of the mob. Screams rent the air.

The panicked, jostling crowd knocked Clemency to the icy ground.

After landing with a sharp jolt, she covered her head and kicked out wildly, trying to clear a space around her so she wouldn't be trampled, but the thundering feet didn't even notice she was there. Boots kicked her back and legs as men shoved each other, scrambling away from the soldiers. Pain pummelled her body, but with a surge of defiant determination, Clemency thrust her hand into the air, reaching toward the sky.

Thirteen

"Clemency!" Arínor screamed, claws of panic ripping her chest and shredding her throat as Clemency disappeared beneath the terrified mob.

She couldn't lose her like she had lost Elandra. She wouldn't lose anyone else to fear.

More shots rang out, followed by the shrieks and wails of colonists beholding the bloody bodies of their dead friends. Arínor's rapid, shallow breaths strangled her, and she coughed, scanning the ground between the jostling legs of the crowd for Clemency.

There. A hand, reaching up toward the sky.

The storm cloud at the back of Arínor's mind roiled and seethed, billowing to the fore and vanquishing all thoughts of her own safety. With a screech of fury, she transformed into a lightning bird.

She had never used her lightning bird form as a weapon before, nor did she intend to now. The Armindí kept their transformations discreet these days, knowing wreaking havoc with their perceived aggressive, combative nature, or causing destruction with storms, was exactly what Carmellians feared. She had no interest in proving them right.

But she *did* have power, and it was time to cease letting fear stop her from wielding it.

Leaping into the air, she pulled her wings in tight and exploded into a rapid spiral, spinning fast like a tornado. Snow and ice rose with her, sucked into the vortex she created, forming a swirling shroud to shield her actions. The crowd gasped and shouted, pointing at the vortex and dispersing like water fleeing a drop of oil.

Arínor dove for Clemency's wavering hand, barrelling through colonists and buffeting men out of the way with her powerful wings, and seized her arm in her talons. Flapping out of the melee, she careened above the mob and over the crimson blood-drenched snow, Clemency dangling from her talons and shrieking. She shot down Crooked Lane and into an alley a few streets away, setting Clemency gently down in the snow.

Dishevelled sandy hair spilled from its pins to flop on Clemency's shoulders. The whites around her cobalt-blue eyes were veined red, raw from tears. Clemency blinked up at the lightning bird looming over her. Fear had vacated her gaze, leaving only awe, and understanding.

"Arínor?" Clemency whispered.

Arínor bowed her feathered head.

"So, you were watching me... following me... making sure I was safe?"

Arínor clicked her beak in confirmation, grateful Clemency couldn't see her blush beneath her feathers. She glanced around the empty alley, then lowered herself as far as she could without lying down, looking pointedly at Clemency—asking her to trust her one more time.

Slowly Clemency rolled to her feet, brushing snow off her body. Standing, she was taller than Arínor as a lightning bird, but Arínor was far stronger.

"Do you want me to... climb on your back? Ride on you?" Clemency guessed.

Arínor nodded.

Reaching out a tentative hand, Clemency brushed her feathers, cradling one between her fingers for closer examination. She ran a thumb over the subtle hints of silver woven in with the ebony gloss, sending a shiver rippling down Arínor's spine.

"It's beautiful," said Clemency, meeting Arínor's eyes. "You're beautiful. I'd be honoured to fly with you."

Hitching up her skirt, Clemency swung a leg over Arínor's back behind her wings and lowered herself gingerly, as though afraid she would be too heavy. She wrapped her arms around Arínor's neck, resting her head between her shoulder blades. When Clemency felt secure enough, Arínor extended her wings and gently lifted them into the air.

Clemency gasped in her ear, squeezing her torso tighter with her knees, but as the wind caressed their cheeks and the snow swirled about them like dancing stars, Clemency squealed in delight, then crowed, throwing her head back, her spirit free and wild.

Weaving through the chimneys and steeples, Arínor wheeled across the town toward the wharfs, searching for an empty one. She spotted one without ships or boats moored abreast of it and descended to land, careful not to jostle Clemency too much as she slipped and skidded on the icy dock. When she found her footing, Clemency dismounted with surprising grace, and Arínor shape-shifted back into her human form.

"That was... exhilarating!" exclaimed Clemency breathlessly, clearly floundering for an accurate enough word to describe the thrill of her first flight. Her chest heaved as though she had just run to the dock instead of hitching a ride on a bird. "I can't believe you can do that!"

"I am a woman of fathomless layers," teased Arínor with a smirk.

"There certainly is no one quite like you," agreed Clemency. Without preamble, she added, "Thank you for saving my life. Again."

"Again?" Arínor repeated, and she could feel her facial features shifting into exaggerated, almost comical confusion.

"There's more than one way to save a life," said Clemency with an indulgent giggle. "Tonight, at the women's meeting, I felt so empowered. Confident in myself, and what I could bring to the conversation. What I could do to inspire others. 'Saved' might be an exaggeration, because I'm pretty damn proud of myself for how far I've come in the last few months, and for all the hard work I've put in. I think I would have found a way to pursue my passions on my own eventually, so I must give myself *some* credit. But it never would have happened in this way, at this time, if it weren't for the way you inspired me. You opened my eyes to possibility and freed my spirit to come alive. I will always be grateful to you for that, Arínor."

Wiping a stray tear from her cheek, Arínor released a throaty chuckle. What had this woman done to her?

"A sentiment that goes both ways, believe me," she replied. "I don't want to be someone driven by fear anymore. You were right. I was always running, terrified of making the wrong decision, so I avoided deciding at all. I feared becoming someone fuelled by hatred, but I avoided my fears and that's exactly what I became. And I almost—"

She swallowed hard, unable to finish her sentence.

"What happened, Arínor? You were attacked, weren't you? By whom?"

"I don't know," admitted Arínor, her voice as heavy as the weight compressing her chest. She looked out at the dark, gently waving ocean, lapping against the dock like the encouraging wag of a dog's tail. "All I could get out of him was Charlotte's father's name and Sampson's."

"Charlotte's father? But—oh." Comprehension dawned on Clemency's face. "Witchcraft. He abhors witchcraft. One of the few people I know who might actually think someone accused of being a witch deserves to die. He must have found out about your magic somehow. Or someone accused you of being a witch."

"That was my general train of thought. You... you didn't..." Arínor wet her parched lips, sure she knew the answer but needing to ask it anyway to calm her nagging doubts. "Did you tell Sampson about my magic?"

"Of course not!" cried Clemency, her pink cheeks draining of colour as she bit her bottom lip. "Did you think I had betrayed you?"

"I didn't want to believe it. I didn't *really* believe it—but I had to ask. You were the only person who knew for sure that I had magic, and you love your husband and trust him. I thought maybe you had told him, thinking he would never do anything harmful with the information, but..."

"Well, if you really believed it, you wouldn't have had to ask, but I guess I understand your doubts. I didn't tell him. He didn't know you had magic—still doesn't. But I am starting to think he spread rumours. I don't think he wanted you dead. I honestly think he's naive enough to believe no one hates witches to the extent of wanting them dead these days. But I know he wanted to sully your reputation so you wouldn't be hanging around so often. He hasn't admitted to using the word yet, but if he met with Charlotte's father... I'm guessing he bandied about the word 'witch,' knowing it would make him determined to keep Charlotte away from you. But I suspect he didn't quite know the depths of William's hatred," said Clemency.

Her downcast head mirrored her crumpled posture, and an unexpected stab of pity pierced Arínor's heart. She suspected their marriage would be as unstable as this icy dock for a while.

"I admit, I came to your house that night wanting to kill your husband," said Arínor, wincing at her blunt delivery but needing to acknowledge her abhorrent actions. "I *acted* like the wicked witches of Earth's stories, consumed by vengeance and rage. But I did change my mind. I came to my senses, came out of the fog of hatred I had been lost to. I wouldn't have killed him, Clemency. I was trying to retreat silently when you came to the door. Can you ever forgive me?"

Clemency didn't answer right away, eyes locked on the undulating black waves. Arínor's shoulders slumped, hunching against the dull but deep ache in her chest.

"You don't need my forgiveness," said Clemency gently. "I think you know from whom you're really seeking forgiveness."

And she did.

She raked her fingers through her tangled hair and rubbed her burning eyes.

Arínor had tried to live a simple life where she could use her Celestial magic, find love, and let the roots she craved grow deep. But it was all an escape, a way to convince herself she had made the right decision by choosing her own life over Elandra's, to make it seem like the sacrifice had been worth it. The truth was she would never live a life she was proud of or found satisfaction and contentment in until she could forgive herself.

Forgive herself for letting her fear control her. Forgive herself for Elandra.

And acknowledge that it was all right to change her mind about what she wanted in life. It was acceptable to want something more. She could choose her happiness, even if what defined her happiness changed. She knew that sometimes sacrificing her own happiness would be necessary, but valuing her life and basing decisions on that was all right too.

Sniffling and wiping an errant tear dangling from her chin, Arínor took a deep breath and squared her shoulders.

She was done running away from her problems. Away from the darkness inside herself, the shadows she feared. It was time to confront them and forgive herself for her flaws, her mistakes, and her imperfect decisions.

"I have to return to Arwé," announced Arínor, new-found purpose steeling her resolve.

Clemency's sigh weighed her whole upper body down. "I feared as much."

"I value our friendship so much Clemency, and would love to stay for that alone. But I'm just in the way here. Without me around, you can be free to fight in the movement against the British with the tools at your disposal as a woman, and not be associated with witchcraft. You can repair your relationship with Sampson without me as a constant wedge between you, and he can give you the support you deserve. One day you could even wage a war against female oppression. You wield your wit and intelligence as weapons and don't need me around to succeed in that."

"Or you could stay and fight alongside me," said Clemency.

"I don't belong here," said Arínor, shaking her head. "Maybe I don't belong in Arwé either, but I know the cause I need to fight, and it's not here on Earth. It might not align with a 'good' direction on a moral compass. But it's the path I need to take."

"I'll miss you," said Clemency fiercely, enveloping her in a hug.

And Arínor could feel the weight behind the words, the layers of unspoken truths.

"I'll miss you too."

Arínor flew Clemency back to Crooked Lane to meet Sampson, who Clemency claimed must be frantic with worry by now at not finding her. Sure enough, when Arínor had deposited her gently in an alley nearby and flown to a rooftop to ensure Clemency reached her husband safely, she saw Sampson run toward Clemency as soon as she turned the corner onto Crooked Lane. His shoulders shook with sobs, the only sound in the now eerily still, silent air.

When Clemency was enfolded safely in Sampson's arms, Arínor flew out over the ocean, seeking the portal she had entered through.

It was time to ascend to heights she was willing to fall from.

Fourteen

Beholding the jagged crown of Harth's snow-capped peak as she flew back through the portal elicited the first tears Arínor had ever shed as a lightning bird. She hadn't even known she could cry in this form, but tears wet the downy feathers surrounding her eyes all the same, and her chest ached so deeply it felt hollow.

This is where she belonged. *This* was home.

But she couldn't return to her cottage. Though she yearned for her family like a parched, wilted plant longing for the rain, she knew if she saw Kat practising his camouflage, or Aríetté with Anya on her hip, or her ma fixing the wagon's wheel, she wouldn't have the courage to make the sacrifice she knew in her heart to be the right path for her. She would stay in that cottage forever, taking root like an ancient eldrin tree.

Careful to keep her back to the direction of her cottage, Arínor sped past the last outcropping of Harth's sharp teeth, blasting a cloud of misty snow into the air, then shot toward Tor Stella Lalíté, wasting no time in searching for the person she needed to instigate her plan: Invidia.

She knew Invidia lived along the shore of the lake, but before she could try to figure out which home belonged to her, she spotted her walking out on the thick ice near the shore. Diving toward Invidia, Arínor swooped across the lake, shape-shifted in mid-air—and broke the ice as she landed, plunging into its freezing depths.

The frigid, wintry water stole her breath, and for a second, she just floated beneath the ice, wrapped in a cold blanket of shock. But as she started drifting, she kicked hard to the surface, her voluminous skirt billowing around her, and broke free of the ice. Gasping to fill her burning lungs, Arínor heaved her sodden, heavy body out of the water, spluttering and cursing, and collapsed onto the intact ice.

"That was quite the entrance," said Invidia.

"Well, I've been away for a while," panted Arínor when she could breathe again. "I needed to make a statement."

"Job well done, then," said Invidia, smiling despite her indifferent tone. "And welcome back! We weren't expecting you for a while yet. Your ma said you were visiting a family friend in Lothilya."

Arínor managed to keep her face blank.

"Yes, that's right. The visit ended early."

Violent shivers racked Arínor's whole body as she lay soaked on the ice.

"Here, let me help," offered Invidia, and a moment later Arínor's shivers had ceased, her clothes dry as a desert. Warmth spread from her chest to her fingertips and toes, like basking in the warm summer sun. She must have used Fire magic.

"Thank you," said Arínor, grateful even if Invidia hadn't bothered to help her escape the icy lake.

"So, what brings you here? Testing your tolerance for pain by jumping into freezing bodies of water?" Invidia asked conversationally.

"Actually, I'm here to let you know that I've thought about what you said in our last conversation before I went away, and I want to join Vashi."

Silence's forked tongue slithered out between them, tasting the air. Invidia's eyes widened as her brows furrowed in suspicion. "Why? Why did you change your mind?"

It was a valid question, one Arínor had expected, but she gripped her elbows and looked out at the frozen lake, contemplating a different answer from the one she'd prepared.

"Do you ever just think, 'I'm never going to get this right'?" said Arínor. "I'm never going to make the right decisions, or say the right things, or be able to accept my mistakes and forgive myself. Maybe growth is just a construct, a concept people cling to so they can feel better about the horrible people they are, because there's the hope they will atone for it later. Or maybe there is growth, in small ways, but not enough to break the cycle of bad decisions and regrets. If there's no growth, though, what do we make decisions for? Maybe I'm just tired of always trying to make the right decision, only for it to turn out to be the wrong one. Maybe I can just make the decision that's best for me in the moment and be happy with that. You were right about fear of the unknown being the greater enemy. I think joining Vashi and fighting against that fear is the decision that's best for me right now. And maybe that's enough of a reason."

Half-truths. That was the key.

Nodding slowly, Invidia tucked her short ebony hair behind an ear thoughtfully and said, "I see what you mean, and I'm sure that will be enough of a reason for Vashi. I think he would be thrilled for you to join him, regardless of the reason."

"Because of my Void magic? Is that why you left this for me?" Arínor asked, pulling the white-and-gold petal out of her pouch. "Vashi knows about how I've been experimenting with Void magic for healing and creating life and wants me to do that for him."

Invidia beamed, as though proud of a student for exceptional research. "That's right! I may have mentioned I had a friend skilled in Celestial magic, and your unique application of Void magic came up. He seemed very interested in it."

"What does he want me to do with it?" Arínor asked, brushing past Invidia's betrayal in mentioning her name as a potential recruit to the most hated man in Arwé.

Invidia pinned her with a long, calculating look.

"You're shrewd," she observed after a minute or two, "which will serve you well with Vashi. I can't say much of what he's doing or your role in it, both because I don't know many specifics myself and because he would kill me if I divulged the little I do know of his secrets without permission. But since he wants you to join him, and you've decided to now, I'll just say that he seeks to bind together a Celestial object, and he believes your affinity with Void magic to heal and create will help bind the pieces together."

Hope soared in Arínor's chest. Her plan might just work.

But she couldn't do it alone.

She needed another Celestial magic wielder.

Luckily, she didn't have to look far.

Kerena answered the tentative knock on her door with an ecstatic grin plastered on her face and a gleeful squeal, launching herself at Arínor for a hug.

"You're here! You're home! You just vanished without saying goodbye. I was worried because it's so unlike you, but Gertie assured me I needn't fret. How are you? Come in for some tea, and tell me all about your visit!"

Arínor accepted the offer, following her inside her bright cottage to a square table painted yellow. With a mug of Kerena's hot, citrusy tea clasped between her hands for courage, Arínor told Kerena everything—where she had really been, why she had left, and what she had realized she needed to do now.

"I may not belong on Earth, but I know I still don't fully belong here in Keleb-Sola either. My Celestial magic and lightning bird shape-shifting paint me as a unique target among the Armindí, and it will just continue to worsen as Vashi's powers grow. Anyone with Celestial magic is at risk right now, but my affinity with Void magic is drawing extra attention, both from those who fear it and those who admire it—like Vashi."

"Vashi knows who you are?" Kerena asked faintly. "He knows of your Void magic?"

"And wants to use it for his own purposes. He's trying to bind together pieces of some Celestial object, and he thinks my unique approach to using Void magic to create instead of deprive will help him achieve this. I think that was the real reason for the attack on my family's home, the reason I'm being targeted instead of you right now. Vashi wants me to join him, and my family will be in danger until I do."

Kerena cupped her hand over her mouth and slowly shook her head. "Oh, Arínor, what will you do? You can't be thinking of joining him."

Arínor tugged on her nose and rubbed her fingers over her cheekbones, then sighed and settled for a sip of her tea. "I don't want to. I'm aware of the heinous acts I will be associating myself with, and the thought doesn't warm my heart. But sometimes the path worth taking, the sacrifice worth making, is the least palatable. The one with the most potential for regret, but also the greatest potential for reward. Not reward for me, but for the people of Carmelle. People who may otherwise be powerless against Vashi's tyranny."

Clemency's face swam in Arínor's mind, her fierce determination and fiery eyes when she took a stand against British tyranny, wielding her quill as a sword to give hope to those who felt powerless to stop it.

"I don't know what this Celestial object does, or why he wants to bind the pieces, but it's obviously important if the choices are death for my family or helping him," continued Arínor, her voice hardening into a steely-edged sword. "And if I join him, I can bring him down from within. I can sabotage his plan with this Celestial object while appearing to help him. But I can't do it alone. Which is where you come in."

"Me?" Kerena's violet eyes widened, horror lacing the dilated fear. "Arínor... you're talking about joining Vashi, the evilest man in all of Carmelle. You may be fine with tossing aside your morals, but I'm not. I can't... I can't join him, even if it is to thwart him. The thought of committing heinous acts doesn't just freeze my heart; it shatters it."

Pressing her lips together in a thin line, Arínor nodded to herself and muttered, "Too much. It's too much to ask, I know. I'm sorry for suggesting it, Kerena. You're right. This is my sacrifice to make, not yours. I'll take my leave now. Thank you for the tea."

Arínor scraped back her chair, shuffled across the room, and reached for the door.

"What would I have to do?" Kerena asked, her resigned voice halting Arínor's hand.

Arínor swivelled, studying the grim set of Kerena's mouth. "Vashi doesn't know about the Armindí's curse magic, or at least if he does, he won't know what it can do, and won't be expecting us to use it. I will help him bind his object. Do what he asks and save my family. But we can tamper with the binding. Curse the pieces so they won't properly coalesce, though they will appear to. The binding and curse will need to be performed congruently, but I can't do both at the same time. I need another Armindí there to curse the pieces while I bind them. An Armindí who also wields Celestial magic, so they have a reason to be there."

For a few long minutes, Kerena picked at a splinter in the table, peeling a pale gouge in an otherwise pristine swath of yellow.

"Tessa and her baby were threatened, you know. While you were away. They're fine," Kerena added quickly at Arínor's gasp. "They weren't attacked like your family. But villagers heckled them outside a shop one day. Said Tessa had better watch out if her sister didn't stop plaguing them with her Sun magic. They weren't even outsiders; they were Armindí. Our own people. But fear for Celestial magic knows no borders. You're right. There aren't a lot of paths left for us. Maybe it's time to be proactive, and protect by attacking, not defending. If we have the power to thwart Vashi, to help end this prejudice against Celestial magic, even in a small way, then it's our duty to try."

Arínor rushed back across the room and squeezed her friend in a tight hug. "I'd want no one else by my side, building Vashi up to bring him down from within. If we're going to be labelled wicked, we may as well embrace the title and use wickedness for good."

Before they met Invidia that night for their journey to Vashi, Arínor had one more person to visit.

She found Gertie melting ice from her front stoop with a thin flame of Fire magic. Her wiry charcoal-grey hair draped across the thick shawl wrapped around her hunched shoulders. Watching her fondly for a moment, Arínor waited until she had melted all the ice before clearing her throat.

"Hi, Gertie. I'm back."

Gertie jumped, unbalancing herself a little as she jerked around to face Arínor.

"Arínor!" she exclaimed. "What are you doing back here?"

"It's nice to see you too," said Arínor, amused sarcasm dripping from her tongue.

"I'm sorry. I'm just surprised," said Gertie, squishing her in a hug. "I didn't know if you would ever come back through that portal, let alone this soon. I assume you're about to tell me why."

"That's why I'm here, yes," confirmed Arínor. "And I can't stay long, unfortunately."

Gertie studied Arínor's face, peering into her eyes as though she could read her soul. Arínor squirmed a little, not entirely sure that Gertie *couldn't* use the deep pools of life experience brimming in her ancient eyes to read her soul. The woman was a never-ending scroll, unfurling a little more of herself every time Arínor thought she had reached the bottom.

"You haven't seen your family. You're not planning on staying."

It wasn't a question, but Arínor shook her head anyway.

Sighing, Gertie waved Arínor inside.

"Better come in. This has all the markings of a conversation that requires sustenance to get through. Have you eaten anything?" Gertie asked, already bustling to gather a random assortment of fruit and nuts and shoving them on the table in front of Arínor.

"Not much. Just a bit of tea at Kerena's," Arínor admitted as her gurgling stomach lurched. She helped herself to some nuts. She was reluctant to burden Gertie with her plan but figured Gertie was the least at risk of retaliation if Vashi should find out what Arínor was doing, and she needed to ask one last favour of her.

"I can't return to my family, Gertie," she began, making a pattern with the nuts on the table to distract her twitching fingers. "They're not safe with me there. *I'm* not safe there. Celestial magic wielders aren't safe anywhere in Carmelle—except with Vashi."

Gertie froze partway through peeling a green kwaka fruit. "You're joining Vashi."

Again not a question, but Arínor still answered. "Yes, but I'm not joining him because I agree with his views or wicked practices. I know rumours are only half-truths and people tend to assume the worst about the other half, but I genuinely believe Vashi is evil, and I don't want to help him take over Carmelle. I'm joining him to help save Carmelle."

"Well, there's a riddle. You're going to have to help me answer this one," said Gertie.

"Sorry, but that's the only answer I can give you. For your own protection."

Gertie sighed, rubbing her smooth eyelids. "All right, so you're going to save Carmelle by destroying it, but you can't tell me why, and you need a favour. What could the favour possibly be?"

Arínor pulled a few of her own black lightning bird feathers out of her skirt pocket and fanned them out on the table in front of Gertie. "I need you to give these to my family. I know Ma has been telling people I went to visit a family friend in Lothilya. I don't know what you told them when I went through the portal, but I think Ma at least still believes I might come back. Once I join Vashi, I can't return. But I don't want them to think I'm dead. I'd like them to have these, as a token of hope. Hope for the well-being of our family. Hope for a better future for Carmelle. And hope that maybe one day families won't have to be torn apart like ours because of prejudiced fears of the unknown."

Gertie picked up the feathers with a surprising gentle reverence, then pocketed them and nodded. "That's a favour I can grant. But, Arínor, remember martyrdom is not a virtue. Your worth is not measured by how much you sacrifice. Knowing your limitations, understanding your own worth and placing value in who you are laid bare of all expectations and pressures, is a strength. When it comes to making sacrifices, it's not how many you're willing to make but knowing which ones *need* to be made, and understanding the full weight of *why*."

Arínor clasped Gertie's long-fingered hand. "I know, and I don't intend to become a martyr. If Kerena and I do this right, Vashi will never even know we've sabotaged him. I never used to understand that about sacrifices, the full weight of the *need* and the *why*, but I think joining Vashi and walking the narrow, precarious line between good and evil is one I need to make. I was meant to do this. I can feel it."

"I believe you were meant for this as well, as much as anyone is meant for anything," agreed Gertie, cupping her cheek tenderly and sharing a sad smile. "You have been adaptable and flexible, adjusting to the new paths your decisions and uncontrollable circumstances have forged, and now this path is laid before you, and I do believe it's one you need to tread. Just remember to keep your feet, and if you lose your balance on that line between good and evil, be wary of which side you fall on."

Arínor lay on her back in the shadow of one of the massive roan peaks of the Dharlomin, refracting moonlight off the twinkling stars with her magic in a dancing light show. All around her, other Celestial magic wielders did the same, painting the sky with broad, shimmering strokes of silver and pearl and white, swaying and whirling them in a moonlight aurora. Beside her, Kerena's violet eyes sparkled, mirroring the stars, and her wide, childish grin spoke to the deep contentment welling in Arínor's soul.

When Invidia had informed Arínor and Kerena two months ago that they would be travelling to a secret stronghold in the Dharlomin mountain range, northwest of Caris Nando, tingling nerves had racked her whole body. She hadn't known if she could play the part of loyal servant to Vashi as convincingly as she would need to, and Invidia would not be staying with them, though she assured them she would check in from time to time. Without Celestial magic, she wasn't much use to the Dharlomin contingent and was needed elsewhere. Arínor had panicked a little when Invidia had left, assuming the followers she would share the stronghold with would be despicable people.

But they weren't, at least not to her. They had been grouped with other Celestial magic wielders, and most of them were outcasts like Arínor and Kerena, fleeing their homelands because of rampant fear and violence toward Celestial magic. On the surface, most seemed nice—pleasant, even—and they shared more similarities than differences. The magic of Sun, Stars, Moon, and Void bonded them, and they discussed theories and possibilities for Celestial application, testing them and creating beauty together. For the first time, Arínor felt truly free to be herself. Free to shed the weight of expectations, shed the regrets of her past, shed the stress and worries of shouldering other people's fears.

She could just be Arínor, and not hold anything back.

Maybe she *was* a witch, and this was her coven.

Jeza, one of the leaders of their Celestial group, plopped down beside Arínor, her crimson cloak pooling across the snow-dusted roan rock like blood. Though the leaders of the group, the ones closest and most loyal to Vashi, were generally callous, Arínor found Jeza to be blunt and brisk but not mean-spirited.

"Tomorrow, some of us are heading to Skeletal Moon Lake, to conduct a ritual for Vashi," Jeza announced without preamble. "All over Carmelle, our fellow Celestial magic wielders are being wrongfully imprisoned, and this ritual will free them. We believe your Void magic will repair a weapon we need to achieve this. Will you help us free them?"

Arínor's stomach flipped, suspecting this weapon was the Celestial object Invidia had referred to, and this was in fact a more important ritual than Jeza was letting on. Whether it would help free other Celestial magic wielders, she didn't know, but she would not sacrifice this opportunity to help all of Carmelle for the benefit of only a few. The stakes were too high.

Keeping her face carefully neutral, Arínor nodded and replied, "I would be happy to. Can Kerena come too?"

Kerena sat up, her face an inscrutable mask. "I would love to help free our wrongfully imprisoned allies as well."

Jeza flicked her gaze between them, considering, her face unreadable.

"We would be honoured to have you join us as well, Kerena." She stood to leave, then paused, peering down at them. "I should mention that this ritual will involve a sacrifice. Are you both prepared for that?"

Though Arínor could hear Kerena gulp, they both nodded in unison. They had always known Vashi's use of Celestial magic demanded blood sacrifices of life and limb, and though Arínor hoped neither of them would have to be the one delivering the killing blow, they were prepared to sacrifice their morals, and perhaps souls, to participate in and witness the ritual if it meant they could curse the object and thwart Vashi's plans, for the greater good.

"Until tomorrow, then." And Jeza left as abruptly as she had arrived.

Arínor slid her hand slowly across the snow to intertwine her fingers with Kerena's.

This was it. The start of their rebellion.

So far, she had seen no sign of Vashi himself. That honour seemed to be reserved for only his closest allies, which suited Arínor just fine.

She could thwart his plans from the shadows without ever having to meet him.

The next evening, Arínor and Kerena met a dozen other Celestial magic wielders at the mouth of the mountain's stronghold. Large crimson cloaks cocooned their bodies, the hoods drawn up so they couldn't see each other's face. Though Arínor knew Kerena stood beside her, she couldn't be sure of the other members' identities. The anonymity prickled her skin, though it was probably just ceremonial.

Three people stepped forward and joined hands. Though Arínor couldn't see what they were doing, she could feel her core surge—a sensation she had developed over the last two months as more people had wielded magic around her. When her swooping stomach stilled, a simple circular portal had opened in mid-air. The edges shimmered and sparked, and through it she could see the same roan-red peaks of the Dharlomin, but this time with a frozen lake nestled between them.

One of the three who had cast the portal stepped through first, and the rest of them followed. A full moon shone overhead, reflected on the surface of the frozen lake. Silently they positioned themselves around the lake, spaced out evenly so they almost formed a semicircle.

Arínor glanced surreptitiously around the clearing, her vision limited by her lowered hood, but saw no bound and gagged prisoners or unconscious bodies for the sacrifice. Perhaps the unfortunate soul would arrive after the ritual had already begun.

"Welcome," Jeza's voice boomed, "to tonight's ritual. The pieces of the weapon, please."

The cloaked figures to Jeza's right and left stepped forward, producing chunks of hardened lava from beneath their cloaks and placing them on a large boulder at the foot of the lake.

Arínor frowned at the pieces, and to her left she noticed Kerena shifting a little.

This was the Celestial object Vashi wished to bind and wield as a weapon? Had they made a terrible mistake?

"Now join hands, and embrace your cores," instructed Jeza.

Arínor obeyed, clasping hands with the people to her left and right and embracing her magic.

Immediately her core pulsed and blazed with light, strands unravelling and floating, unbidden, toward the lava pieces, drawn by a greater power. Arínor gasped, desperately trying to rein them in, to regain control. Closing her eyes, she breathed deeply and focused all her energy into pushing the errant strands back into a sphere. The lava pieces continued to beckon, to draw her magic to them. Beads of sweat trickled down her forehead. Her arms shook, and she squeezed the hands she held harder. They tightened their grip in return, and Arínor noticed most of the figures trembled around the semicircle.

A hidden power radiated within the hardened lava pieces, commanding and insatiable. It felt fathomless, akin to the emptiness of a void, but teeming with potential, like a life about to be created. All doubts vanished from Arínor's mind: this raw power would make a terrifying weapon in Vashi's hands, and she knew she must carry out her plan and stop the binding from coalescing properly at all costs.

"Everyone but Arínor, call on the pull of the moon to fit these pieces together," commanded Jeza. "Arínor, use your creation Void magic to bind them."

As one, the group drew on the full moon's pull, fusing it with their channelled magic to lift the lava pieces into the air and fit them together. When they melded together so she could barely see the seams, Arínor plucked a strand of Void magic from her core and took a deep breath, attempting to calm her thrashing heart. Concentrating on filling and creating, not emptying and deprivation, Arínor reached out not only to the hardened lava but to the unseen power within the pieces as well. The power threatened to overwhelm her, pulling on her magic like an insatiable void, but Arínor pushed back, concentrating on redirecting that fractured, ravenous hunger inward, folding it in on itself. She melded it together with a magical sealant, creating an impenetrable bonding agent of light and... was that... stardust?

Sweat poured down her face now, stinging her eyes and salting her tongue, and her chest heaved, straining with the effort. Energy drained from her body as if it were a sieve, depleting the strength in her muscles, her bones. But still she held on, thinking of Clemency's wild, empowered laugh.

Beside her, Arínor heard a barely audible murmur from Kerena as she muttered the curse under her breath, and though she couldn't feel the curse, she knew in her gut that it worked its way into the sealant she was creating—cursing the binding with a promise of breaking.

At last the binding was complete. Arínor released her core, stumbling sideways, starlight winking in her blurry vision. She squeezed her forehead between her fingers, willing her vision to clear.

When the mountain peaks and frozen lake finally came back into focus, she saw only Jeza and Kerena, still holding her hand. Kerena's hood had lifted a little, revealing her quivering chin and lips.

A chill ran down Arínor's spine and lifted the hairs on her sweaty neck.

"Wh-where is everyone?" Arínor stuttered.

Hands seized her from behind and threw her forward, wrenching her hand from Kerena's.

Her elbow smacked against the ice as she landed on the frozen lake, fracturing her bone, but not the ice. She tried to lift herself up and screamed in agony as pain lanced her wrist and shot up her forearm. Blood pounded in her ringing ears, and she blinked blurrily at the shore.

The cloaked figures had connected hands again, a wall of blood against the stark white snow-capped peaks. Magic thrummed between their connected hands, faster and brighter.

It was time for the sacrifice.

And *she* was the victim.

Arínor tried to stumble to her feet, but her exhausted, depleted legs wouldn't support her.

She embraced the storm cloud at the back of her mind, letting it roil to the fore so she could shape-shift into a lightning bird and fly away—but a gnawing emptiness consumed her core, and she faltered, looking down.

A yawning black hole gaped in her midriff, bleeding outward, eating her insides with a thousand sharp, unseen teeth.

If pain hadn't been burning her throat and charring her lungs, she would have laughed.

Void magic, in its darkest, basest form.

They had needed her to bind, but they had no trouble tearing her apart.

In a last act of defiance, Arínor thought of her ma's comforting arms, Gertie's gumption for hard truths, Aríetté's selflessness, and Clemency's fervor for freedom. She filled her soul with the comfort of her family's hugs and the warmth of their eyes, and the promise of Clemency's lips. She poured all the love she had experienced in her life into her soul, knowing Vashi's followers were about to empty it and feed it back to the stars as stardust.

She screamed as the pain peaked, shredding her skin and muscle from bone, shrieking until blood gurgled in her throat, and someone screamed with her on the shore, sobbing her name—

And then the pain ceased.

The void's gaping maw swallowed her, and she floated into its vast ebony emptiness.

A daughter of darkness, lost to the shadows.

Epilogue

October 29, 1770, Salem, Massachusetts

Wiping a tear from her smooth cheek, Gertie ran a finger over her daughter's name on the cold gravestone:

Nonie Browne Anderson
1688–1739

She must have married, then. Maybe had children of her own. But she had died so young… Sobs burned Gertie's throat again, and she swallowed them down, breathing deeply through her nose. If she dissolved into any more hysterics, someone would fetch a doctor. She had always known she would outlive her children, being an immortal Armindí, blessed—or cursed—with the gift of time unless disease or a fatal wound befell her, but it seemed so short a time for her sacrifice to have bought them.

Sandwiching Nonie's tombstone on either side were her parents' graves. Her darling Abner's on one side, the date indicating he had lived until around seventy, and Gertie's own untimely grave on the other, bearing her full name: Gertrude Browne.

Abigail's name was nowhere to be seen on the surrounding tombstones, which meant either her eldest daughter was still alive or she had been buried somewhere else.

A biting autumn breeze nipped Gertie's ears, and she wrapped her wool shawl tighter around her shoulders.

"Cold day, isn't it?" a friendly voice asked behind her.

The sound of dead leaves crunching carried on the wind, and Gertie turned to see a woman with sandy ringlets and cobalt-blue eyes walking toward her.

"I should really wear more layers, but I never remember to," said Gertie. "Here to visit someone as well?"

"My grandmother," the woman replied, coming to stand beside Gertie. "My husband has been stuck working in Boston for almost a week now. My kids are occupied for the day, and my best friend is busy supporting her husband during the biggest trial of his life as a lawyer, so I decided to take a trip to Salem and visit my grandmother's grave. It has been a long time since I've been able to come here. I guess Salem has been on my mind a bit more lately, what with my friend Arínor—"

She paused, shaking her head as though admonishing herself for rambling to a stranger, but Gertie's eyes widened, her heart galloping like a unicorn's thunderous hooves.

"Did you say Arínor?" Gertie repeated faintly.

"Yes, Arínor," the woman confirmed, her lips quirking in the corners a little. "Unusual name, I know."

It couldn't be the same Arínor. Of all the people Gertie would run into on her first day back on Earth, it couldn't be someone Arínor had met while here. Fate was not that cruel. Or kind.

"Arínor from... Arwé?" Gertie ventured, figuring she had nothing to lose by throwing the name out there. If this woman didn't recognize it, she would just think it was somewhere on Earth she hadn't heard of, or that Gertie was crazy.

Now it was the woman's turn to gawk.

"You know about Arwé?" she gasped.

Apparently, fate didn't give a damn about her conflicted feelings. Though Gertie had learned that lesson long ago, it still always surprised her a little how accurate the Armindish way of life was. Sometimes you truly did stumble upon the right path for you at the right moment without knowing it.

"I'm from Arwé as well," said Gertie. "And Arínor was a close friend of mine."

"Was?" the woman repeated, her brows furrowing.

Grief sliced through Gertie's heart like a dagger at the memory of receiving Kerena's letter. She still didn't know how the girl had managed to sneak a letter to her while among Vashi's followers, and she hadn't included any details of Arínor's death. Just that she had died in the service of Vashi, followed by two words: *It's done.*

Gertie guessed Kerena hadn't wanted to say too much in case the letter was intercepted, but she had deduced that "it's done" meant Arínor had completed her mission to save Carmelle by joining Vashi. Which made her a hero in Gertie's books.

"What's your name?" Gertie asked the woman.

"Clemency," the woman answered slowly, confusion misting her eyes.

"I'm sorry to tell you this, Clemency, but Arínor has passed," Gertie informed her, voice trembling despite her best efforts to steady it.

A guttural gasp of pain wrenched itself from Clemency's lips, and she doubled over as though she had been punched, reaching out for something to steady her and finding Gertie's arm.

"I'm sorry," Clemency whispered, righting herself and releasing Gertie.

"Don't be. I take it you knew Arínor well?"

"She was like a sister," choked Clemency.

Gertie enveloped this stranger in a hug, rubbing her back in soothing circles, her gut twisting at the girl's obvious pain and sorrow. She let

Clemency cry for a few minutes, then spoke into the silence. "I don't mean to take away from your grief, but I won't lie. It does me good to see someone who cared so much about Arínor, outside of her family. How did you become friends?"

Clemency straightened from Gertie's embrace and dried her eyes on the sleeve of her dress. "She defended my honour as a woman and first introduced me to the idea of taking a stand against the mistreatment of women in our world. She made it seem so easy, like equality should be as easy as breathing. It inspired me."

Gertie smiled, warmth spreading from her chest to her fingertips. "That sounds like Arínor. She was an inspiring woman."

It was after she had relayed the news to Arínor's family that Gertie had decided to come back to Earth, inspired by Arínor's renewed determination and purpose upon her return. The idea of returning to Earth had been too painful before. She couldn't bring herself to watch her children grow without her, or find out if Abner had remarried, or watch her children die and be able to do nothing. It had been better to slam the door and keep it shut.

But after Arínor's death, she had started feeling like she needed closure. She had felt enough time had passed that she could return and mourn with discretion. And she had feared if she waited too long, she wouldn't be able to transform into a lightning bird anymore because of the pain in her bones from countless years of shape-shifting, and therefore wouldn't be able to fly through the portal.

"You know, I daresay Arínor was inspired by her time on Earth as well," said Gertie after a few minutes of Clemency's hiccups and sniffles. "She came back to Arwé with renewed purpose, and she died fighting for a cause she believed in. I think she might have achieved something quite important for our world."

Clemency beamed through her tears. "I knew it. I knew she'd make herself proud. I know I'm proud of her."

"Me too," Gertie agreed.

"She saved my life, you know," said Clemency after a moment, brushing her boot lightly across the spray of vermilion and ruby leaves adorning the graves. "The night she left Earth. There was this awful riot. Five people died, six more gravely injured, and I was nearly counted among them. Arínor transformed into this huge black bird and saved me without a thought for her own safety."

Tears pricked Gertie's eyes again, and she blinked them away stubbornly.

"They called the riot that night the Boston Massacre in the papers, after Paul Revere's bloody engraving of the attack," Clemency continued. "It ignited a spark in the conflagration of revolution. The Townshend Acts were repealed shortly after, and the British captain present at the shootings was just acquitted. It's only a matter of time now until there's a revolutionary war. That's what my play's about. The one I started writing when Arínor was here. I just finished the first draft. It's a satiric tragedy of revolution."

Gertie arched an eyebrow. "Well, that sounds interesting. Do you have plans to do anything with this play once the final draft is complete?"

"I'm not sure yet," said Clemency, her gaze drifting to the trees. "I might try to publish it. Arínor always encouraged me to use my voice, even when men said I shouldn't. She knew someone who needed to hear it would always be listening, and it would inspire them."

"Clemency," Gertie began, reaching into her pocket for Arínor's last lightning bird feather. "I think you should have this. I was going to keep it for myself, but I think Arínor would want you to have it."

Eyes widening, Clemency cradled the feather in her palm, stroking it tenderly. "This is a feather from Arínor's bird form. I can't... She gave it to you..."

"She would want you to have it," Gertie insisted. "Turn it into a quill. Give your voice power through words, and use the pain of the past to right the wrongs of the future."

Clemency hesitated a moment more, then clutched the feather to her chest.

"Thank you," she whispered.

Gertie put her arm around Clemency's shoulder, and they stood there in silence for a while, content to share in each other's grief and relive memories of Arínor. A tune floated across Gertie's mind, one she had locked away long ago. She hummed the first few notes, then sang softly:

> *Daughter of darkness, for you there is light,*
> *Wherever you go, even in the darkness of night.*

An old Armindish lullaby, sung to young Armindish girls, the daughters of darkness. It had fallen out of fashion in the last half century or so, since "daughters of darkness" referred to their evolution from lightning birds, and fewer Armindí could shape-shift these days. But Gertie had always loved it and had found new meaning in its verses for her children.

"My grandmother used to sing me that song," said Clemency, eyes alight with wonder. "The one whose grave I'm here to visit. I've never met anyone else who knew it."

Gertie stopped breathing, frozen in this moment of epiphany.

"What was your grandmother's name?" she whispered when she could breathe again. But she didn't need to ask. She already knew.

"Nonie. That's her grave, there," Clemency confirmed, pointing to Gertie's daughter's.

Heart aching and eyes watering, Gertie clutched her chest, bracing against the waves of joy and sorrow washing through her.

"So, will you go back to Arwé now?" Clemency asked, oblivious to their connection.

Their kinship.

"No," said Gertie, smiling through her tears. "No, I don't think I will. I'm finally home."

Author's Note

Thank you for reading *A Tragedy of Sacrifice*. If this is your first immersion into the world of Arwé, I hope it has inspired you to read the rest of the series.

One aspect of this story I wanted to highlight to readers is the fact that the fictional character of Clemency is based on a real person in history: Mercy Otis Warren.

For those unfamiliar with Mercy Otis Warren, she was a writer, political playwright, poet, and intellectual in the American Revolution era, living from 1728 – 1814. Her and her husband James were Patriots, and engaged socially with some of the most prominent political figures of the day, including John and Abigail Adams, Martha Washington, and Samuel Adams. They hosted the Sons of Liberty in their Plymouth home, and James supported and encouraged Mercy's political writing. Mercy boycotted British imports and encouraged other women to do the same, and balanced political writing pursuits with raising her five sons. Though she was not formally educated herself, she believed women should have the opportunity for formal education instead of having to teach themselves. After the Boston Massacre, Mercy wrote and anonymously published (anonymous because she was a woman) a political tragedy, a play called *The Adulateur*, in which she indirectly criticized Governor Thomas Hutchinson for the way he handled the Boston Massacre and predicted the American Revolution. At the encouragement of her close friend John Adams, she wrote a history of the American Revolution while it was still happening, and later published it under her own name in 1805. It was entitled *History of the Rise, Progress and Termination of the American Revolution.*

While Clemency's story is not intended to be a biography of Mercy Otis Warren, or be completely accurate to every aspect of her life, as she is her own character with her own dreams, aspirations, and fears, I was inspired by Mercy and decided to base Clemency's character on her, striving to reflect Mercy's life as closely as possible within the context of my own story. I hope I did Mercy justice, and that readers will see Mercy reflected in Clemency and be inspired by the real-life inspiration behind Clemency's character.

If you would like to learn more about Mercy Otis Warren, here are a couple of resources to help you get started:

Michals, Debra. "Mercy Otis Warren." National Women's History Museum. National Women's History Museum, 2015. Accessed September 2024. https://www.womenshistory.org/education-resources/biographies/mercy-otis-warren

Stuart, Nancy Rubin. *The Muse of the Revolution: The Secret Pen of Mercy Otis Warren and the Founding of a Nation.* Beacon Press, 2009.

I know time is precious and leaving reviews can be daunting, but I would be ever so grateful and honoured if you would consider leaving a review on Goodreads or Amazon. Other than purchasing a book, leaving a review or rating helps support an author, and will help other readers find the book and decide whether they want to read it. And I of course value and appreciate your feedback.

If you are already subscribed to my newsletter, thank you so much for subscribing! You can look forward to exclusive updates on the world of Arwé soon. If you are not subscribed, I encourage you to consider subscribing through my website at www.kayleaprime.com. Through my newsletter, you will be privy to monthly writing updates, first announcements about upcoming books and cover reveals, ARC opportunities, and other exclusive content. You'll even receive a FREE exclusive ebook of my prequel novella, *A Ballad of Hate and Hope*.

You can also find me across most social media platforms under the handle @kayleaprime.

Thank you again for your support!

-Kaylea Prime

Map of Boston, 1776

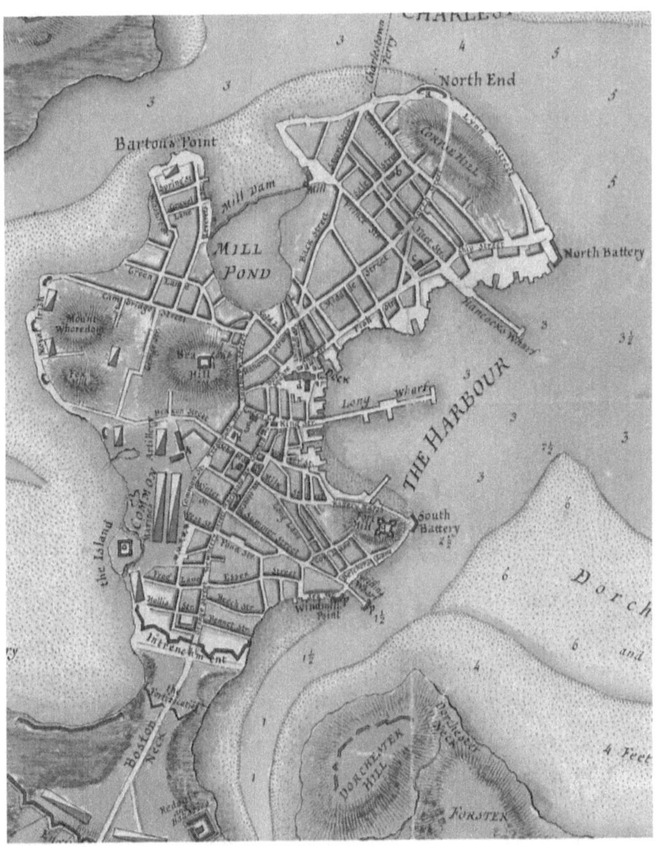

Page, Thomas Hyde, Sir. A plan of the town of Boston and its environs, with the lines, batteries, and incampments of the British and American armies. [1776] Map. Retrieved from the Library of Congress, <www.loc.gov/item/gm71000622/>.

Acknowledgements

Sometimes a story calls to you, clamouring to be told, and you know deep in your soul that you need to heed that call before writing anything else. This was *A Tragedy of Sacrifice* for me. The idea for it had been percolating in my mind for some time, bubbling and simmering until it coalesced into an elixir ready to drink, and I couldn't ignore the temptation. It's probably the most personal story I've written, tackling themes and subject matters that felt very cathartic to write.

Just as Clemency acknowledges her own strength and the role she played in the growth and achievements she experiences in this story while still thanking Arínor for inspiring her, I too feel like I need to acknowledge my own strength and courage in facing some of my fears and sharing such a personal story. I'm proud of myself for taking the cathartic writing journey I needed to embark on at this time in my life. As Clemency and Arínor taught me, if you want change, you have to inspire it. I hope that this story inspires even just one reader.

So much of this story was about forgiveness. Forgiving others, but most importantly, forgiving ourselves for the mistakes we don't think we can live with. None of us are infallible, but mistakes are not just about fallibility. Sometimes our regrets are a reflection of the fact that we have changed and grown as people. A decision that you later regret doesn't necessarily mean it was the wrong decision to make in the moment. Our wants and needs change as we evolve, and a decision we made based on the different needs of our past selves is no less valid because we might make a different decision for the same circumstance today.

This story is also about sacrifice. Knowing when to make them, and why. Sometimes our sacrifices ring hollow and feel like they're for naught, but sometimes even the small sacrifices can have a huge impact.

Thank you to everyone who made small or big sacrifices to help me write and publish this book, and thank you to everyone who helped me learn to grant myself clemency, starting with my husband, Sid. You have made many sacrifices to ensure I can continue pursuing my writing dreams, and I'm so grateful. Your support through the most difficult times of my life meant everything, and I was able to find the strength to write this story because you helped show me that I could chase away the shadows with my own light. That my feelings were not only valid, but could change as I changed, and that was valid too. You are my ever-fixèd mark, and I miss you, always.

Thanks to my parents, Sylvia and Ron, who gave me the roots Arínor always craved. Over the years, you've granted me more clemency than any one person deserves, but also taught me the meaning of forgiveness, both for the importance of forgiving others, and forgiving myself. You have been there for me through every moment of regret and triumph, and have sacrificed more for me, my happiness, and the pursuit of my dreams than anyone. Words cannot express the love and gratitude I feel knowing that you will always be there for me, unconditionally.

Thank you to my sisters, Candace and Tamara, for listening without judgment, always showing empathy and understanding, and for making our bonds of sisterhood so strong. Growing up, I always knew I had my sisters. I could confide in you both, share my fears and doubts, and count on support, even if our opinions differed. I love that I can still come to you now and feel like you're my safe space, but also sources of inspiration. Motherhood has demanded sacrifices from us all, but the grace with which you both rise to the challenges constantly inspires me, and I am often in awe of you both. You are both strong, capable, intelligent, compassionate women, and Clemency and Arínor would be proud to welcome you to their sisterhood. We're like the three Schuyler sisters from Hamilton! *Work!*

Thank you to my wonderful daughters, Jade and Eralyn, for pushing me to be the best person I can be by virtue of your very existence, and continuing to inspire me to write stories that I hope will one day inspire you, in turn. I never thought I would write such feminist-centric stories, but it's so important to me that you feel empowered, and I hope characters like Arínor and Clemency help you feel you can inspire change in yourself and the world. Thank you to Eralyn as well for the excellent cat names (Tundra and Moonstone).

Thank you to Bethany, my friend, critique partner, and only alpha reader of this story. I literally could not have written this book without you, and I certainly could not have published it in the timeframe that I did. Your endless, unwavering support blows me away, and I am so thankful that we found each other on this crazy writing journey. Getting to read your stories has been an absolute privilege, but the greater privilege is getting to be your friend. Our little witch coven of two is the best found family ever. You are one of the most inspiring women I know, and I'm so honoured that Arínor and Clemency have inspired you even a little in return.

Thank you to my copyeditor, Leonora, for your astute insight and impeccable attention to detail. I am in awe of your keen eye, and your dedication to historical accuracy is so crucial for a historical fantasy writer.

Thank you to my cover design team at Miblart for another stunning cover. I think this might be my favourite one yet. I don't know how you get my vision so exactly right every time, but I am so grateful to be able to give my stories the dream covers they deserve.

Thank you to Mercy Otis Warren for challenging societal gender norms over two centuries ago, and proving women had the intellect and savvy to ensure their voices were heard in meaningful ways. Your legacy inspired

Clemency's character, and inspired me. Thank you to all the contemporary women writers out there as well, who continue to inspire people with their words.

Thank you to my four-legged companions, my golden retriever dogs Marvel and Lily, who may as well be emotional therapy dogs for all the snuggles and love you indulge me with when I need them most. And thank you to my writing buddy, my cat Sir Copper Neutron, who blocked me from my keyboard, demanding chin scratches, and curled up by my warm laptop, typing random words with his errant paw. I suppose your deafening purrs were cute once you actually stopped blocking my keyboard and graced me with your indulgent presence.

And of course, I must thank Arínor, Clemency, and Gertie. I know it might be odd to thank your own characters, but these three special women kind of wrote themselves, taking me along for the ride and inspiring me along the way with subtle strengths and acts of courage that I didn't even know I needed to experience until writing them brought me to tears.

And most importantly, I would like to thank you, my dear readers, for stepping through the portal to Arwé with me again and giving a new set of characters a chance. I hope you enjoyed Arínor and Clemency's story as much as I enjoyed writing it.

About the Author

Kaylea Prime is the author of the fantasy series, *Tears of Flame*. She is also a librarian with a passion for planning epic programs that immerse kids and teens into their favourite literary worlds. When she's not writing or working as a librarian, she can be found exploring the beautiful wilderness around her home in Clearwater, British Columbia, with her two kids, husband, and two golden retrievers.

@kayleaprime
www.kayleaprime.com